Malbister

An NC500 Road Trip Adventure

Julie MP Adams

Copyright 2020 Julie MP Adams

The moral right of JMP Adams to be identified as the author of this work has been asserted in accordance with the Copyright, Designs and Patents Act, 1988.

All rights reserved. No part of this publication may be reproduced or transmitted in any form or by any means, electronic or mechanical without permission in writing from the publisher.

This book is a work of fiction. Names, characters, businesses, organizations, places and events are either the product of the author's imagination or used fictitiously. Any resemblance to actual persons, living or dead, events or locales is entirely coincidental.

ISBN: 9798577449094

Dedication

To my mum and dad – who always believed in me.

Chapter 1:
On the Road

June 3rd, 2019

The estate agent, a sniffy young madam called Shelby, was on my doorstep at ten am prompt. She pulled an iPad from her Louis Vuitton Never full tote. Whatever happened to a plain clipboard and checklist? Or to a plain handbag without a flashy logo?

I'd been up half the night scrubbing, wiping down surfaces and steam cleaning the bathroom tiles. I'd finished at five am and sank into my sleeping bag on the floor, utterly exhausted. The house looked good though. It was a damn sight better than when we'd moved in five years ago.

She shook my hand. Her manicured mitt was silky smooth and she'd had her gel nails done. My paws were wrinkly, red raw and my contact dermatitis was making a comeback, despite the rubber gloves I'd worn to do the get out deep clean. Shelby did offer me the use of their agency cleaner, but he came at the cost of my deposit, and right now I needed every penny I could get.

Julie MP Adams

The storage company lockers were priced according to size – small – enough for the sentimental rubbish I couldn't bear to part with, was fifty pounds a month. The bigger size, which would fit my furniture was four times that sum. Heaven only knew when I'd get a roof over my head again—it would either need to go into store—or I'd need to part with it. Over the last fortnight I'd packed from dawn to midnight, and when I wasn't packing, I was flogging my furniture on Facebook Marketplace. I'd hoped to keep my bed until this morning, but the couple who bought it turned up last night instead, because they couldn't get the van today. Fair enough, I thought as they handed over their hundred quid in used fivers. I'd paid ten times that amount for the mattress alone only eighteen months ago.

Shelby had the decency to attempt to look vaguely apologetic. 'The buyers will be here at midday, if you want to get yourself some breakfast while I'm doing the inventory.'

'What? And mess up the kitchen I've been cleaning?' I snapped. Besides, I'd had my breakfast – a single digestive biscuit and a cup of coffee. It was just as well Kevin wasn't here—he'd have insisted on his full English, messing up the hob and splashing grease on the worktop.

Shelby trotted from room to room. Her heels were an inch too high and I could see the red soles of her shoes. She must be on a decent commission to afford those, I thought. She wore the estate agent's uniform – charcoal grey skirt suit, the skirt bit being a little too tight, to show off her curves. She wore a lanyard and had a photo ID on it—Shelby R Russell, and some letters after her name from a professional organisation. Every so often she raised the iPad and took a picture.

It wasn't our first meeting. She'd done the six-month inspection three months ago. She'd pointed out a couple of

Malbister

scuffs on the paintwork, which I'd promised to do something about. I told Kevin about that later and he exploded. 'I suppose you did tell her the place was a tip when we moved in, and that it's our carpets and our wallpaper?'

Shelby was a new girl. Her predecessor, Irene, knew all about the work we'd done on the house, and the reason why our rent used to be low. The first week after Irene retired, the letting agents doubled what we paid each month.

She was speaking. Her mouth was moving but her words weren't actually sinking in. It was something about white goods?

'We put the kitchen in ourselves. My husband got the built-in appliances at trade discount. I thought you were going to give us something in lieu of the cost?'

'I'll have to ask my boss about that.'

Her phone rang out, and she said, 'Excuse me, I'll have to take this,' and trotted through to the empty sitting room. I could see her through the glass doors that divided the sitting room from the kitchen. I'd hoovered the carpet and used the Vax on a couple of marks. The Vax was inside Morag, ready to go back to Dorothy, before I hit the road. The venetian blinds were staying—anything that was fixtures and fittings, even those belonging to me, would be staying put. They probably wouldn't fit anywhere else, anyway.

I looked at her with her designer handbag and her Louboutin shoes and for a moment I felt a stab of envy. There was a small solitaire diamond on her ring finger, and she had that smug smirk of someone who is getting things all her own way. Was I ever like that?

She returned to the kitchen. 'I asked about the appliances and getting some money for them, and the boss says it's no can do, I'm afraid.'

Finally, she handed me the iPad to check and sign. 'I

want the deposit to be refunded to my account—the rent always comes out of my account, not the joint one,' I said, firmly.

'Do we have your forwarding address?' she asked. 'I didn't see if you'd rented something else from us.'

I pointed out of the window to where Morag was parked along the street. 'That's my address for the foreseeable future. You can get me on my mobile, or on email.'

She looked down at the iPad again and realised she'd said something tactless. Kevin, of course, had an address.

I went upstairs to take a last look around, and looking at the indentations on the carpet, despite the ice cubes I'd put on them last night to raise the pile, I burst into tears. I looked at the mirrored wardrobe doors, ours, bought at trade prices and hardly recognised myself. I'd washed my hair before I'd blitzed the bathroom and tied it back. I had no make-up on, and I looked a decade older than forty-five. I had jeans and a t shirt on, and worn ballet flats on my feet. All my smart clothes were in storage now, apart from a few bits and pieces in Morag's tiny lockers. My wedding ring was in my purse, ready to pawn, along with my other bits and bobs.

Finally, I handed her my keys. Kevin's set was on the kitchen worktop, and I pointed it out to her. Her phone rang again, and I made that the excuse to slip away.

I got into Morag, settled myself into the driver's seat and put my seatbelt on. I checked my mirrors and pulled away carefully, driving to Dorothy's house across town to return her Vax. She asked me in, and refused my excuses. 'Wendy, it's not as if either of us has anything to rush for today. The least you can do for me is keep me company for a few minutes and help me eat some of these.' She indicated the tower of chocolate boxes on her kitchen table.

'Everyone had the same idea about what to give me as a

Malbister

leaving present,' she said. 'I don't even like chocolates that much.'

Dorothy's house was pristine if old fashioned, and her kitchen was a haven of comfort, with a range cooker and a scrubbed pine table. She spent much of her time in there, and she turned down the radio and put the kettle on.

I sat on a kitchen chair and her dog sat beside me and offered me a paw. 'You're honoured,' Dorothy said, as she spooned coffee into a cafetiere and poured milk into a frothing jug. She put two Denby mugs on the table, poured boiling water into the cafetiere and brought it and the jug to the table. She waited a moment before pressing the plunger down and offered it to me to pour. Meanwhile she opened one of the chocolate boxes and pushed it across to me.

'How was it? Leaving the house?'

I shrugged. 'It was only a rental, so I shouldn't get so upset.' A gulp and I realised I was sobbing again.

Give Dorothy her due, she knows how to deal with people. She pushed a box of tissues in front of me and said, 'Take your time, Wendy. You've had a lot on your plate. I've got a spare room if you want it – just to let you get back on your feet?'

I shook my head. 'If Kev sees Morag on your driveway, he'll only come and take her, and she's all I've managed to hang on to.'

'How are you fixed for money?'

'I've got enough for a couple of months. I'll be fine,' I said.

Two hours later, I climbed back into the driver's seat. I'd convinced Dorothy I knew what I was doing. Now I needed to convince myself.

Chapter 2

7th March, 2019

'Mrs Latimer, could you come through to the office for a minute?' I wondered about the formality. Dorothy always calls me Wendy, even on the shop floor. She's on first name terms with all the department heads, which is probably why we've not looked for work elsewhere. Fisher and Gregory employees in our town branch are pretty loyal.

I checked myself in the mirror beside my position and topped up my lipstick from the sample that Geraldine from Estee Lauder gave me last week. Then I checked I had my keys with me and went through.

I wasn't expecting to see the HR people from Head Office. We'd not had word of a visit, and normally we know three days in advance, so one of us can pop to the baker's in the High Street to order their lunch for them. It's usually my job if it's HR – Fenella McGilp is a coeliac and I need to make sure her filled roll is gluten free.

There they were, sitting behind Dorothy's desk: no Fenella but three men in dark grey suits, with iPads and clipboards.

Malbister

'Ah, Mrs Latimer?' the first grey man looked up from the clipboard. 'Now this is nothing to worry about...'

I started to worry. It's how Matthew's teachers always began an interview at Parents' Night, if he wasn't doing well.

The second grey man, who looked as if his collar was a bit on the tight side, continued: 'You've probably heard in the media that our parent company is undergoing a restructuring process, mainly due to the rise of internet shopping impacting on the high streets. We're looking at how each of our stores is performing and getting a picture of the people who work in the shops.'

The third not so wise monkey in grey delivered the punch line. 'There will be closures, inevitably. However, it is not yet confirmed where these will be. There will be some flexibility for people to move to another store if their one closes.' That would be alright for Dorothy—she's a widow and her only dependent is her poodle. I tried to think how Kevin would feel if I had to drive fifty miles to Swindon, six days a week.

'I see you've been with us for fifteen years, Mrs Latimer,' the first one said. 'And you've held a junior management position for ten years? Have you never wanted to move on with your career?'

I could see the calculator on the iPad tabulating fifteen weeks salary. Department store pay is never just about the salary—it's calculated with bonuses. In a good year, my bonus is as much as my pay. I squinted at the screen. £6000 wouldn't go far, not with a daughter at university and a son on his post grad gap year.

'I love working here. It's a great store and we have a strong customer base. There are generations of people who have shopped here for decades. It will kill the High Street in this town if we close. There are lots of other businesses that depend on us.' I was being too defensive, and they probably hated that.'

'My dear Mrs ...err... Latimer,' the second one said, glancing at the list in his hand, 'When JTC Holdings took over Fisher and Gregory, we knew the firm was over extended. Not all of the stores had consistently strong performance, and we are moving towards merging with our other businesses.'

The third stuck the knife in: 'This is a courtesy visit to allow junior managers time to begin to prepare their CV's ahead of any closures.' He nodded, and said to Dorothy.' Mrs Kent, can you send the next one through?'

My mouth was dry, and my head was pounding. My hearing switched off, and I sleepwalked back on to the shop floor. I wondered which poor cow had the job of buying lunch for those three? I'd be tempted to stuff it with a dose of laxative, or hemlock, if the health food shop sold it.

One after another, I saw the other department heads do what I'd done, innocently smartening themselves up, painting on the bright customer relations smile, and going through, only to return with slumped shoulders and an invisible knife between their shoulder blades.

The sales team on my floor – the beauty concessions and the jewellery departments – went on with their jobs. At lunch time, people from offices and banks come in. They try the perfume testers and speak to the girls at Estee or Urban Decay or Dior about what mascara to buy or which gift set to get for Mother's Day. If we offer them the right sort of service, they go upstairs to buy shoes or a frock for the wedding they've been invited to, or wedding gifts. We know our jobs—we pull in the punters and we set them on a carefully calibrated escalator of spending. Our town isn't a major city, but the High Street here does better than anything

Malbister

else near us. We'd heard the rumours about restructuring, but we'd been a bit too smug. Now it looked as if we were wrong about everything. Geraldine came over at 2pm, before she went on her break. 'Everything okay?'

I tried what I hoped looked like a genuine smile. 'Of course,' I said. 'Was that Mrs Couper you were with?'

She gave an impish grin. 'Just sold her the entire new collection. Sent her away happy. She's gone up to buy new underwear. Said she has a hot date.' She winked, knowingly. Geraldine has a customer file that goes back at least a decade. She knows her customers' likes and dislikes inside out. She knows who is about to get married; who is divorced; who's a new mum; who has a parent in hospital; who's had surgery. Mrs Couper's one of her regulars – a divorced business woman with deep pockets.

Tony, from Urban Decay, was doubling up with the Dior girl, to let her on her break. He lay in wait for the guys from the solicitor's office, and sprayed scent onto slips of card. 'Mum's Day smellies?' he simpered. It worked. When I checked, our takings were satisfyingly up. Surely we could ride this out?

By half past three, the grey monkeys departed, and one after another, we slunk back into Dorothy's office, to get her take on what was going to happen.

This time, there was a big box of tissues on the coffee table with the soft seats ranged around it. I mentally labelled it the crying corner, because when she sat there, it was usually because someone was either getting a tactful bollocking, or was upset over something serious. I took the seat on the other side of the L from her.

'Look,' she began, 'I'm sorry about this, but it's as much of a shock to me as it must have been to you and the others.'

'Why are they picking on us?' I asked. 'We've always

done better than the other stores. You know that—the proof's in our bonuses.'

She shook her head. I looked at her sharp bob. I'd not noticed the grey strands before. She looked a decade older than she had this morning. 'And therein lies the rub. The holding company were after the buildings – not the business, when they took us over. They mentioned they have prospective buyers, but they want vacant occupancy. You of all people, should know how that works.

'So, what happens to us?' I said, noticing my voice now sounded like a pathetic whine.

'People like me will be offered early retirement to get shot of us. I'm lucky that I'm close to my pension age, and I've got the lump sum from Arthur's pension,' she said. I mentally added, and a house with no mortgage and probably savings.

'You're a young woman, Wendy,' she said. 'Look at any package they are offering. You could retrain? You've got a degree, after all. They're always looking for teachers or civil servants. Or you could look for a manager's job. You're more than qualified for that, and you know I will give you a glowing reference.'

She was trying to make me feel better, but I burst into tears. She moved across and sat beside me, pulling a tissue from the box and handing it to me. Then she put her arm round my shoulder and gave me a brief, fierce hug.

I pulled away with what I hoped looked like a smile. 'I'd better ask Geraldine to give me a makeover before the late opening customers come in,' I said. I went down to the shop floor telling myself it was going to be alright, but without conviction.

Chapter 3

I put Morag into gear and drove carefully on the A roads north, avoiding the motorways. I looked for a big branch of Tesco, one with a filling station. My plan was to head north, away from Gloucestershire. I'd calculated that if I put cheap fuel into Morag, and drove gently, I could afford to book us into a campsite every few days.

I'd already filled the water tanks, and there were the remnants of the fridge contents in the kitchen lockers. In the passenger footwell was a box filled with dry goods – instant coffee, tea bags and plain biscuits.

Morag's been part of my life for at least a decade. Kev used to say that we couldn't have two cars and Morag, so I gave up my Corsa, and used Morag to do the food shop on my days off.

She's a motor home – the smallest you can get with a loo and shower. Right now, she was my home. I'd applied for a business management post grad course, which JTC Holdings were graciously funding as part of my redundancy package. It was due to start in September but until then, I'd need to find some temp work. I reckoned I was due a holiday so without any clear idea in my head I was going to keep on the move and try to focus on seeing a bit of the country and hopefully picking up a bar job somewhere along the route.

It was the first time in my life that I'd been entirely alone.

Chapter 4

I knew all too well about how property developers work.

When my kids were small, I did the admin for Kevin's business. Dad used to go on about my wasting my education by marrying my first boyfriend and giving up my own career to help build his. I'd left a good job with prospects in London to come back to my home town and marry a small-time builder.

To be honest, while Kevin was a small-time builder, we were actually okay. He bought cheap plots of land, applied for planning permission and built timber framed bungalows on them. He used other self-employed trades – Smudge the joiner; Arthur the sparkie; Hawkeye the plumber. Their dads put them through their apprenticeships and there was rarely a time, even in a recession, where they didn't have work. Back in 2008, when things were tough, they did nothing but garage conversions and kitchen refits. Nobody starved.

I liked our first house. It was nothing great—a semi-detached in the outskirts that we did up ourselves. I had Matthew, and then Amy, and I did the books for Kevin and the lads' businesses while my babies were having their naps or in the evenings, after they'd gone to bed.

Julie MP Adams

Kevin has old fashioned views for a man of his generation. He likes to be in charge, and to make all the decisions. One day he came home to tell me he'd sold our house. 'Listen, Wendy, I've got a great plot looked out, and there's a kit for a five bed with a double garage that'll be just right for it. The couple that wanted this one paid over its value—it means we'll have a smaller mortgage and a bigger house.'

In reality, it meant I took two small children to live with Mum and Dad, while Kevin camped out in Morag on the site. Granted it was summer, and living in Morag the campervan was a practical way of avoiding wasting money on rent, but Dad was furious. 'That bloody brickie takes you for granted and us for mugs.'

Kev did the same thing twice while the kids were at primary school. Then he got ideas above his station. The lads – Smudge, Hawkeye and Arthur, and Kevin – mortgaged all their homes to buy a derelict mill, with the intention of creating ten luxury apartments. The plan was for us all to move into the development, and have the business office in the outbuildings on the site. He promised me a desk and a computer and a show home to tempt customers. I told Dad, as we moved in for what was to be the last time, that the business was on the up.

Kevin and the boys were sold a pig in a poke. The company selling the site didn't bother to mention it was Grade Two Listed, and that there were bats in the roof cavity. They applied for planning permission over and over, and it was consistently knocked back. Hawkeye's wife left him, saying that she wasn't prepared to live in a static caravan on site, which was what we were all faced with when the bank called in their loans.

To get a roof back over our heads, I needed a job that

Malbister

wasn't linked to the business. Round about the same time, Kevin was declared bankrupt and I said I'd pay the bills for the place we had to rent. I temped for a bit, often in call centres, then Mum tipped me off about the job in the department store. She'd worked there for years when I was growing up, and I was used to dropping in just before closing time, when I was a teenager in school uniform. She put a word in for me with the manager before Dorothy and I got taken on as a temp at first, but then I started to work my way up. She helped me out by picking the kids up from school when they were small and when I got home after work, there was usually a meal ready to put into the oven.

Dad still grunted at my lack of ambition, but when there are four mouths to feed, there's not the time to go back to Uni to do the Masters in Business Management – which all of those vacancies said was essential.

I got into a daily routine. I'd be up at six to get pack lunches ready and to get into the shower before Kevin and the kids used up the hot water. I'd check school uniforms were clean and I'd go through the schoolbags with the timetables to make sure they had clean gym kit, or an apron for Home Ec. I'd get breakfast on the kitchen table, and then I'd nip back upstairs to whip the rollers out of my hair and get my make up on.

I'd take a look in the bedroom mirror at my smart self with well-groomed hair and make-up in the navy-blue dress and jacket, and then put my heels in my handbag and put on the flat shoes I wore to get to the bus stop to catch the 27 into work. The doorman was there to let us in before the store opened, and we'd exchange a word about the weather or the news, before I went to the staff room to put the flat shoes into my locker, with my handbag. Heels on, and keys clipped onto my jacket, I'd check my appearance in the mirror, then go down to the shop floor, to get a spray of whatever perfume we were promoting that week.

I worked long hours, but I enjoyed my job, and I got promoted to section head after two years. My wage paid our rent, our food and the utility bills, and while Kevin grumped, at least I had Dad off my back.

Lately, things picked up a bit at home. The lads had to walk away from the mill—it was repossessed by the bank, and we'd been through the horrors of bankruptcy. But now, they were back building bungalows – admittedly as employees of a bigger company – and we were talking about having a place that wasn't rented. The catch was that it would need to be my name on the mortgage, and I needed my job, if I wasn't going to be another statistic on Universal Credit.

The rest of the day dragged, and one after another, the women I work with dropped by to ask why the section heads all looked as if the earth had opened up. Dorothy had pleaded with us not to make it common knowledge, but Lydia in soft furnishings had been in tears and Stu, her assistant, wormed it out of her. Since he's known for exaggeration, they'd come looking for confirmation. All I could say was that there was some restructuring planned, and I knew nothing more than they did.

It was late closing. I'd rung Kev to tell him to order our takeaway pizza, but he didn't pick up. I wasn't worried – if he's on a roof, banging a nail into a slate, he knows to wait until he's on ground level before checking his messages. He usually sends me a text to ask what toppings I want, but today, he seemed to have forgotten. I was on the rota to help lock up, so I couldn't skive off to check my phone, and the next time I remembered, I was on the 27-bus home.

I pressed call and it went straight to voicemail. 'Hi, you've come through to Kev Latimer's phone. Please leave a number and a message and I'll get back to you.' He must be in the shower, I thought. He'd been working on site all day, and he'd be cleaning up before I got home. I hoped he wasn't going to head for bed straight after our supper. The doctor had told him off about eating before bedtime. I'd got used to adding Rennies and Gaviscon to the weekly shop, but I mentioned it to Dad and he scoffed and said, 'That brickie you married wouldn't recognise a bus if it was about to hit him head on – let alone a heart attack.'

I felt guilty now about ordering pizza. If I was a proper attentive wife, I'd have left a salad for him in the fridge on Thursdays.

I sent a text. On bus – see u soon x.

The bus stop is two blocks from our place. It started to rain as I got off the 27 and I hadn't got my brolly with me. I started to walk smartly, hoping I wouldn't get soaked through. So, I didn't notice Kevin's truck wasn't outside our door. I did notice that the place was in darkness. Surely, he wasn't in bed already? Or had he come home and decided to go out again? Once inside, I hung up my coat, turned the lights on in the hallway and in the kitchen, and nipped upstairs to take off my work clothes and get into the pyjamas I wear when I'm home for the evening. Then I checked my messages – nothing.

I rang the pizza delivery place and asked about our order. It turned out that nobody had taken the order, so I asked for a large thin and crispy Margherita and a side order of garlic bread. I rang Kev's phone again, and just like before, it went to voicemail.

I was worried. Surely, if anything had happened, someone – police, hospital, or whatever, would have contacted me by now? I wondered if he'd maybe lost his phone, so I rang Smudge.

Julie MP Adams

'Hi, Smudge. It's Wendy. Were you working with Kev today? I've been trying to ring him and his phone keeps going straight to voicemail.'

The voice at the other end sounded odd. 'Hi, Wendy. Why would Kev be working with us? He said he was taking some time off a couple of weeks back. Hasn't he been doing a homer on the Couper estate job? He said he'd be back in touch when it was finished.'

I hung up and went through to the cubbyhole under the stairs we use as an office. I switched the laptop on, and checked the invoices. The Couper estate sounded familiar, but usually when Kev took a side hustle on, he told me about it, in case he needed me to order up materials or work out how to bill it.

I didn't find an invoice. Only a post it, with an address and a mobile number. Margaret Couper 07766 433190. I rang the number and it was picked up after it rang out five times. There were voices in the background and the woman who spoke had been laughing at something. 'Am I speaking to Margaret Couper?' I asked

'This is she,'she replied. Her voice was annoyingly posh.

'Mrs Couper, I believe my husband has been doing some building work for you, this week? I'm trying to contact him and he isn't answering his phone. Is he working late?'

'You could say that,' she said. The voice in the background mumbled something, and there was the sound of a door slamming and an engine starting.

'Can you ask him to call home? I'm worried about him.'

'Actually,' she said, 'he's just left. He mentioned that you work late today and I offered him dinner. I'm sorry if that wasn't convenient.' Her voice wasn't just annoyingly posh— it was infuriatingly smug. Worse still, I knew exactly who it belonged to. Hot date my foot!

Malbister

My pizza arrived three minutes before Kevin's van drew up and I heard his key in the lock.

He called through 'That's me back now. Alright if I nip up and shower? The lady of the house gave me dinner when I said you work late today. I won't need anything just now.'

'Can you come through for a second?' I was out of my seat and barring his way to the stairs in an instant. I grabbed him by the collar and took a deep sniff. He reeked of Margaret Couper's perfume. Beige—one of those Chanel Les Exclusif scents that cost almost two hundred pounds. And there was a trace of her Estee Lauder lipstick on his neck.

It wasn't the first time he'd been seduced by the lady of a house. The mill fiasco after all was a deal with a couple who owned it. The lads were remodelling the stable block in their Cotswold manor house and Lady Caroline had asked Kev to do some additional work on her dressing room. The mill was her husband's revenge, but it was Caroline who sweet talked Kev into getting his best friends to give up their family homes for nothing. I'd hoped he had learned his lesson. Clearly, I was wrong.

He pulled away from me and climbed the stairs, while I sat down on the sofa and opened my pizza box. It was my favourite, but I might as well have had a slice of buttered cardboard in front of me. I managed a slice before I had to dash to the loo to throw up.

I washed my mouth out and went back to make a cup of tea. I put the remains of the pizza into the fridge—it would have to do for Kev's lunchbox tomorrow—provided Mrs Couper wasn't offering pesto paninis and beer. I went to the door to check it was locked and put on the chain. That was when I saw the envelope in the mail box basket. I took it out and groaned. It had the letterhead of the letting agent. They'd done the six-month inspection, so it couldn't be that. When I saw what it contained, I sank down onto the lowest tread of the stairs. The agent, Irene, gave us a decent deal on our private let, after Kev's deal went sour and I was back living with Mum and Dad. The woman who owned the house lived in Scotland, and inherited it from her parents. It hadn't sold and she'd asked the agent to find a tenant until the market picked up. We'd promised to do it up for her if she lowered the rent, and we'd kept our word and looked after it. In fact, the agent – Shelby, not Irene – said at the last inspection it was as good as a new house. So good that someone asked if it was coming back to the market and we had notice to quit.

Kevin was up to his old tricks. My job was on the line, and we were going to be homeless. Could this day get any worse?

Chapter 5

Work was buzzing with rumour the next morning. Our email inboxes had a template for a CV and there was a link to an online course on interview technique and CV preparation, courtesy of JTC holdings. News filtered down to all of the staff, including the cleaners. The doorman was anguished when I arrived. He'd been with the department store all his life, man and boy. He was well past retirement, but we all reckoned that the job kept him going. HIs wife was in a care home, thanks to dementia. 'Looks like I'll have to take up playing bowls in the daytime,' he tried to joke, but his eyes were moist and his voice quavered.

    The customers were aware of what was going on. Mrs Pilkington, seventy if she's a day but looks twenty years younger thanks to weekly facials and visits to the hair salon on the top floor, handed her stylist her card and told her to let her know when she set up in business and she would send all her friends to her. At least Kelly and Jasmine could be self-employed—their skills could go anywhere. Jasmine told me she'd be sending her CV to the cruise companies. Why not? She's in her early twenties, single and lives with her parents.

Julie MP Adams

A small, sulky voice I barely recognised inside was wailing 'what about me?'

I'd tried to be rational with Kevin last night. But my mouth was dry and my heart thumped so loudly I knew I'd be unable to sleep a wink. I didn't know which of the three nightmares was the worst? Losing the job was bad enough. The men in grey had a point when they asked why I'd not tried to climb the career ladder. It was less about ambition than it was about keeping my marriage together. If I put my ambitions first, we'd have probably needed to move, and Kev liked his home town and being near his Mum and Dad.

That was always a sore point with my parents. They'd always drummed into me the importance of education. They were delighted when I passed exams and went to University – Dad still has my graduation photo on his sideboard. He doesn't have my wedding photograph though. Since Mum died, he's been on about what a disappointment Kev is. He moved to Spain last year, so that I couldn't move back in with him if things went wrong again.

Kevin is a charmer. I've known him all my life—at nursery school we played together. At primary, he beat off the bullies (including Hawkeye) for me. Our teachers used to joke about the little sweethearts—I did have girlfriends, but I usually walked home with Kevin, unless he was at football practice. We lived in the same street, after all. He's not exactly handsome, but he knows how to make other people feel good about themselves.

Dad reckoned that if I'd left home to go to university, rather than go to the nearest one, I might have outgrown Kevin. As it was, I graduated and took a graduate entry post in an office in London, going back at weekends. I liked my job, and I was good at it. I'd see Kevin when I went home, or he'd get on the train to London and share my three-

Malbister

quarter bed in my HMO room. I wasn't in any rush for things to change, but I missed a period and did a pregnancy test. Mum was in bits when I told her I was going to have a termination, before Kevin found out.

I'd booked an appointment at the clinic for the Wednesday that week, and I didn't sleep a wink all week. I made an excuse not to see Kevin over the weekend. Part of me was thinking I wanted a family – only not yet. I liked my job, and I wanted to keep it, but alone in London with a baby? I'd sobbed on the phone a few times when Mum rang me. On the Tuesday, Kevin came into my office, barging past the girl on reception. He was in his work clothes, and he even had his hard hat on. He arrived at my desk, and went down on one knee. He had a ring—a solitaire diamond that I'd once said I liked when we were passing the jeweller's. Everyone in the office burst into applause when I said yes.

Mum wanted to plan a big wedding, but Dad was furious. 'She's made her bed; she can bloody well lie in it,' he said. I don't know if it was my showing him up by getting pregnant, or that he just didn't want Kevin in the family. 'She could have done much better for herself than that bloody brickie.'

We got married in the Registry Office. I was four months pregnant, but I wore a white dress, and we had a table in Mum's favourite restaurant – just both sets of parents, Kev's brother and sister, and my sister, Kate. Just family.

Next year was going to be our silver wedding anniversary. Whatever I thought life had ahead for us, it wasn't this.

Chapter 6

June 3rd

My phone was on the makeshift stand Kevin had fixed to the dashboard. I was using it as a sat nav, so I let it ring out until I pulled into a Sainsbury's car park, just outside Swindon.

I checked the number—it was my sister Kate. I'd not spoken to her for months. I wondered if Dad told her about me losing my job and about Kevin. Maybe she was ringing to gloat? She was the daughter whose wedding picture *was* on the mantlepiece. Kate is two years younger than me, and everything I got wrong, she got right. I might have a better degree than her, but she made it to senior management and married a rich man. Malcolm Goddard is the polar opposite of Kevin. I doubt he's ever built so much as a flat pack bookcase from Ikea. He certainly doesn't need to.

There was a voicemail message. The voice was mumbling, but I recognised it as Kate's. And she wasn't ringing to speak to me—she was having some sort of row. I heard a muffled scream. And I knew where Morag and me were heading.

Chapter 1

June 3rd 2019

I'd sworn I wasn't going to take Morag on the motorways. She's not one of those huge American motorhomes, like a Winnebago, but she's not tiny either. And she certainly isn't fast. I hate when angry truck drivers pull out to overtake, or I get hooted at for not having the split-second reflexes of a Formula 1 driver. I'd intended to hit the road, and amble my way round the country for a couple of months until my course started, but now, I might need to change my plans.

I told myself that it could all have been a mistake. Maybe it was a butt call—one of those where you accidentally trigger the call function on your iPhone whatever? Maybe she was just watching something on telly with a violent row in the background? Or maybe she was in real trouble and didn't know how to call for help. I sent a quick text:

Hi – its Wendy. Did u call me?

I was in a supermarket car park, and there was a filling station so I filled up with diesel and went into the store to get a couple of odds and ends. It felt a bit unreal to be shopping for one, and avoiding things I'd need to refrigerate.

Julie MP Adams

I dropped a packet of dried pasta and a couple of jars of pesto into my basket, along with some UHT milk and a jar of instant coffee. An assistant with a trolley and labels was reducing the price of bags of salad and some fruit, so I loitered with intent and grabbed what I needed for supper tonight and food for tomorrow. Then I nipped into the loo while I was there, and checked my phone. No message from Kate.

The phone pinged just as I got back to Morag. It was a WhatsApp from my daughter Amy, with a picture of her smiling and tanned outside some French bakery with her basket of baguettes. She'd scored a holiday job in the South of France working for a vineyard that rented out gites. It had been sorted last year, and while we'd told her we'd be moving while she was away, I didn't have the heart to tell her we were moving apart too. Let her enjoy her summer, thinking her parents were okay.

I made my way carefully to Cheltenham where I planned to join the motorway. I tapped in the phone number for Kate, but the call went straight to voicemail. I tried to sound bright and positive: 'Hi Kate, it's Wendy—you know, your big sister, right? I'm having a bit of a touring holiday in Morag and I might drop in on you at some point. Can you give me a call? Bye.'

I stopped at motorway services, grudging the fee for overnight, but reckoning I'd sooner be safe than trying to park up in a layby. I threw a salad wrap together and ate it with a soft drink. I thought about what Kevin might be doing and gave myself a shake. He'd made his choice, and it wasn't his wife or his family. I checked Facebook to see what my son, Matt, was up to. There was a new picture – of him at a dig in Jordan. Only my son could have opted to do a degree in geology then a masters in forensic science and

Malbister

archaeology. His gap year was spent on a series of placements where his skills were required. I drew a deep breath.

In happier times, I'd have booked Morag and all of us into a nice site in Cheltenham and spent a day at the races. Or we'd have gone to Stratford on Avon, seen a play and eaten in a gastropub before falling into our bunks. This was the first time I'd ever spent on my own in almost a quarter of a century. No Kevin, no kids and only myself to please. There was half of a bottle of red wine in the food locker. I poured myself a glass and found my kindle. I'd think about my route north tomorrow.

My phone beeped at 3 am, waking me out of a bad dream. I'd sat up straight, banging my head against the roof. I'd taken the upper bunk, which didn't have much headroom, to leave the seating area free. For some reason, I was uneasy about letting anyone know there was a lone female in Morag.

I scrambled down the ladder and checked the phone.

Sorry for not texting sooner. Would love to see u. Do u know the way to Malbister? K

I sent a quick reply: will be with you Wednesday. W x

A minute later: OK text when u get to Inverness.

I climbed back into the bunk and fell into a deep sleep.

Chapter 8

4th June, 2019

The next morning I woke and tackled the reality of van life. I heated water, poured half of it into a collapsible basin and used a flannel to soap myself clean before rinsing off in the tiny shower. The rest of the kettle I used to make my coffee. Morag's side windows have a reflective film that Kev put on them in one of his upgrades, so I knew I didn't need to worry about people seeing in, as long as I pulled down the blind behind the front seats. Once I was washed and dressed, I pulled the blind back up and looked around me while I breakfasted. I took out my portable mirror and my make up bag and made myself look presentable. I scowled at my reflection. There were new frown lines and my hair, without its rollers and products looked listless and lank. Across the car park, corpulent lorry drivers were easing themselves out of their cabs, heading for the showers in the main block, and no doubt a hearty cooked breakfast. I wondered how people coped living on the road all the time. Just a day in and I was already wondering how I'd survive until September – never mind beyond then.

Malbister

I went outside, locked Morag and went for a short walk across to find a loo that I wouldn't need to empty and stretched my legs for a bit on the way back. I had a long drive ahead of me – on the rest of the M5 and onto the M6, which I didn't relish. Part of me wanted to head off in the opposite direction and park Morag near a beach where I could sit and sunbathe, but if there was something going on and Kate was in trouble, I'd never forgive myself.

To be fair, I'd been annoyed at how Mum and Dad had been prouder of my little sister than they'd ever been of me. I'd held down a job, and my marriage had lasted over two decades, and we had raised two great, well-adjusted kids, while she married at forty, after a string of disastrous relationships. On one occasion, she called Kev to ask him to help her remove a date who had turned nasty from her flat. He came back shaking his head. 'I can't understand why she keeps finding creeps,' he said. The creep – a city trader – had given her such a hard wallop she lost a tooth and had to wear a denture for months while she waited for an implant to settle. Then she met Malcolm Goddard at a conference and four months later she married him in a small service in the Maldives, with only Mum and Dad, and Malcolm's mother and his three kids present. To be fair, we were invited, but the island didn't have cheap flights, and we couldn't afford to go. I hadn't seen her since they moved so far north it looked as if they planned to cut themselves off from us all. I knew she'd taken Mum's death hard, but their move was followed closely by Dad deciding to go and live in Spain, and I felt they'd all forgotten about me.

I was approaching Morag when a voice called out, ' Is this yours?' A man in a white shirt and black jeans, was walking round my van, taking an unhealthy interest in her.

He held out a tanned hand with a chunky gold bracelet

clanking on his wrist. 'Delighted to see one of these old girls still on the road,' he said, grinning. He had a gold filling on an eye tooth, and a gold chain round his neck. He was shorter than Kev and built a bit like a bull, muscular chested. The sort of man who spends at least two hours in the gym doing weights every night, and can't pass a mirror without checking his reflection.

'Yes,' I replied, thinking, 'what business is it of yours anyway?'

'Joe Ricci,' he said by way of introduction. 'I used to work for the company that designed your van. I have to apologise for not giving you a bigger shower—we got that right a year later.'

'We manage,' I said, putting emphasis on the 'we' bit. If this was some sort of chat up line, he'd picked the wrong time and the wrong woman.

He was still nosing around the van, tapping at a patch of rust on the rear wheel arch that Kev had missed on the last coach-building session.

'She's in great shape,' he said. 'You obviously take good care of her. Are you going far?'

'Why?' I knew it sounded defensive, but he seemed to know what he was talking about.

'Your tyres need a bit of air,' he replied, 'And they'll probably need renewing in about a few thousand miles. Stay safe, okay?'

I hesitated then said 'I'm heading up to the North Highlands.'

Again that smile, 'Taking her on the North Coast 500? You and the rest of the motor home world?'

'Visiting family, actually. And not really looking forward to such a long drive.'

He said, 'Wait a minute' and walked across to a flashy red

Malbister

car a few hundred yards away. He returned with a leaflet and a business card, both of which he handed to me. 'I'm heading in the same direction as you, but I have two of these maps. They might come in handy: they give you a list of the places you need to see to make the trip worthwhile. The card has my number. If you ever fancy parting with your van, I'd make you a decent offer, for sentimental reasons. The Vanozza was my first design job. Good to meet you...'

'Wendy. Wendy Latimer,' I replied.

'Drive easy, Wendy.'

And with that he was gone. I saw his car pull out – a Maserati, of course, and he gave me a wave as he passed.

Chapter 9

I reached West Bromwich mid-morning; a bit shaken after seeing a damaged vehicle on the hard shoulder. I'd slowed down automatically and was jolted by a cacophony of trucks and cars all hooting at me, as they were forced to brake. I'm a good driver, but I was terrified by the prospect of navigating spaghetti junction. As long as I kept following signs saying North, I reckoned I would manage. I pulled into the nearest motorway services shortly after one, and made myself another salad wrap. I'd planned to try to get to Perth today, but I was far more tired than I'd bargained for. I decided that Carlisle might be a better prospect for the night.

I checked my phone. The battery was running low and I'd need to plug it into the charger once I got going again. I looked at my Facebook and there was one of those reminder posts, from three years ago. We were at Matt's graduation, my son in his cap and gown, Amy grinning, showing the braces on her teeth and Kev and I dressed in wedding guest mode. That was a good day, I thought. I felt that lump rise in my throat again, and gave myself a shake.

Music, I decided, and rooted in the glove compartment for a CD. There were a dozen in the rack, most of them

Malbister

Kevin's choices – Nirvana, Blur and Oasis. Finally, I found the Eagles Greatest Hits and put it on continuous play. It was Mum's favourite music, and I always thought of her when I played it.

I was glad of the lighter nights, as I pulled into Carlisle in the early evening. I parked up near the castle and took myself for a walk. At least I was getting the chance to be a bit of a tourist, I thought. I'd checked the Lonely Planet guide which pointed out at least four bars or restaurants, none of which I could really afford, but the website said the Cathedral and the Castle were both worth a look. The car park would be locked overnight, but I checked with another van that pulled up and the couple inside – older than me by at least a decade—said they usually parked here on their way north.

I cooked some pasta on the stove and stirred in a couple of spoons of pesto, and added some rocket leaves and a bit of cheese. I dumped it into a bowl, grabbed a fork then I poured what was left of the wine, and checked the phone again.

I suppose it was only natural that I'd want to know what Kevin was up to. He steadfastly refused to use social media, so I looked at Mrs Couper's profile. She didn't mention Kevin directly—only that there was building work going on in her house and some pictures of work in progress. It was an extension – a new wing to an already vast property. Kevin had made the excuse that it was easier for him to live in, to get an early start and work late to crack on with it, but I knew it was an excuse for him to be at the beck and call of a woman I knew went through lovers the way most people go through socks, changing them regularly and discarding when they started to show signs of wear and tear. He spoke of another project starting when this one finished, and I wondered if he was making plans to move in with her permanently?

Julie MP Adams

He seemed bemused when I got upset. We were about to be made homeless and I'd lost my job. Both our kids were overseas, and he was playing around with yet another wealthy client. I had my pride.

'Why don't you go and visit your dad, love?' he'd suggested. 'You could do with a proper holiday, and I could come out and join you after I finish the job.'

I'd rung Dad and asked if I could come and visit and he shocked me by saying it didn't suit him. 'That bloody brickie's back to his old tricks, isn't he? It's time you got shot of him. Put your foot down, let him know he can't mess you around.' He had friends staying throughout June – Mum's best friend, also a widow, and only one guest room. I wasn't welcome, even if, as I suggested, I put up in an hotel.

I'd told Dorothy about it, and she'd offered her spare room, but she'd also suggested I go and see her friend – a retired solicitor who volunteered at the Citizens Advice Bureau, and by the end of the appointment, I realised I had grounds for a separation, if not an actual divorce. We had little savings, and our only assets were a joint account with the savings for a mortgage deposit, my redundancy money, Kevin's work van and Morag. That's when I decided I'd take her on the road, and accept the college place in Sheffield, miles away. The next place I rented would be for one person.

The HR people had suggested I join LinkedIn, as part of my job search, which meant I could look people up. Mrs Couper was on there. I looked down at the list of companies she was involved with and got a jolt to find it included JTC Holdings. The parent company that had made me redundant.

I looked up Malcolm Goddard.

Kate's husband was a hedge fund manager. He'd gone to Eton, Balliol College, Oxford, and Harvard Business School. His background was a world away from ours. He had more

Malbister

in common with Mrs Couper (Cheltenham Ladies College and Girton) than he had with my sister. We'd grown up in a 1960's semi, gone to the local comprehensive school and to the nearest university we could attend without leaving home. We weren't poor, but we weren't rich or privileged either.

I'd met him twice—we'd been invited to a dinner shortly after Katie met him, and later we attended their engagement do, which was held in the Ritz. He struck me as a cold fish, arrogant and aloof. His son was there, and he was barely polite to Kevin and me. It didn't bode well.

I wondered what sort of reception I would get, turning up at his estate: Malbister.

Chapter 10

I took off my make-up, did my night time skincare ritual and washed as best I could, scrubbing myself with a warm flannel, and cleaning my teeth before getting into the vest and knickers that I used as pyjamas, and climbing into my bunk over the driver cabin.

I'd fallen asleep almost immediately. I was utterly exhausted. I didn't realise how stressful motorway driving with a motorhome was for someone like me who had never done it before. Kev always made it look so easy. 'You just need to know where you're going and stick with it,' he laughed. 'No changing your mind halfway round a roundabout or on a flyover.'

The banging on the sides of Morag woke me up. Someone was thumping my van and trying to scare me. I scrambled down and looked out of the side window. The group of louts had moved on to the other motor home. I hoped the couple weren't as scared as I was. I heard barking – of course – they had a dog, didn't they?

It was about two in the morning. Goodness knows if I was going to get back to sleep now.

In my mind I planned my route north. The M6 would

Malbister

take me almost to Glasgow, and another interchange, where I'd need to get on the M8, follow signs for Stirling and get on to the A9. I was thinking about the distance from Perth to Caithness at the point where I couldn't stay awake any longer and drifted into an uneasy sleep.

Chapter 11

June 5th

I did a quick detour to Gretna the next day. I didn't need to—it just seemed a good idea at the time. I wanted a bit of distraction and I found it in the shape of Joe Ricci, whose flashy red car was parked near Morag, in the Blacksmith's car park.

He called over to me, 'I wondered if you and Vanozza were going this way?'

'She's Morag, not Vanozza, to me,' I replied.

'Why?'

We got Morag as settlement of an unpaid debt. Kevin installed a conservatory and a kitchen for an elderly couple back in 2003, but before they could settle the bill, the husband died of a massive heart attack. It turned out that his pension died with him, and while his widow inherited his house, their savings were in a term deposit that she couldn't access until the estate was wound up. It was a considerable sum, and sitting on the driveway was a fairy new motorhome that she was about to try and sell. Kevin could either wait for his money or for the motorhome to sell – or he could take it

Malbister

as payment. It came at the time when Kevin had just sold our home and he was building the next one, and it offered him the solution for where to live while he was working on our site. He'd intended to sell it afterwards, but we used Morag to take our holidays that summer. Amy couldn't pronounce the word 'motorhome' so we gave it a nickname, which stuck.

'Family thing,' I said. 'You can do me a favour. What do you get as a gift for hosts who already have everything money can buy?'

He frowned. 'Alcohol? Unless one of them has a drink problem. How rich?'

'Hedge fund manager rich,' I replied. 'My brother-in-law.'

'If you're heading north of Inverness, there's a few distilleries near the road. Single malt will probably do it – if you can afford it. Otherwise, nip into House of Bruar, and buy some posh olive oil and nibbles. You can't really go wrong with food, unless they're vegans,' he laughed.

I looked in one or two of the shops at Gretna and almost keeled over at the price of the whiskies. This summer was supposed to be about gentle touring and trying to find a bit of casual work. By the time I paid for the fuel to take Morag up to Katie, I'd be running low on funds. I wondered if there might be some sort of seasonal job when I got there.

I watched as Joe Ricci filled a basket with shortbread and oatcakes and added some jars of chutney and jam. He paid with a credit card he pulled from his shirt pocket, and divided his purchases into two bags. He handed one of the bags to me. 'Don't be insulted.' he whispered.

He invited me to join him for coffee in one of the cafes. We found a table by a window and a waitress came over to take our order. Joe peered at the menu before reaching into his breast pocket for reading glasses and with a sigh of 'That's better,' ordered cappuccino for me, a double shot flat white for him and two enormous slices of cake. Sitting across the table from him, sipping at my cappuccino, I was subjected to an interrogation – not about myself but about Morag. How fuel efficient was she? How had the kitchen area stood up to wear and tear? How much work had we done on her interior?

I found myself telling the story about how we'd modified the kitchen, and replaced the upholstery after Amy had been sick during a Cornwall holiday and no matter how much Febreze we used, we couldn't get the smell to go away.

Finally, 'So how come you're on the road on your own this time?'

I gave a carefully edited version. My stuff was in storage, since we were between rentals. I'd been made redundant but had a training course coming up, in a different area. My husband was a building contractor, working on a project where he was living on site. My kids were overseas during Uni breaks. I had family in the Highlands and now seemed a good time to do a catch-up visit. Nothing about my marriage being on the rocks, my job prospects low and the very real fact I was temporarily homeless.

'What's taking you north?' I asked.

'Work,' he replied. 'I'm at a trade show to promote my latest project.'

'A new campervan?' I asked.

He shook his head and drank from his cup. 'I design flat pack holiday homes. Lots of remote areas have a shortage of housing for essential workers because when something comes on the market, it gets snapped up as a second home for a city family with more money than sense, or it gets bought as an Air BnB let. I design holiday lodges and park

Malbister

homes. It lets the Air BnB lot have something low maintenance to rent out without taking a proper house away from a nurse or a welder. I'm going up to attend a launch of our new design in a holiday park near Inverness, then I'm looking at some potential sites around the North Coast 500. You never know, our paths may cross again, Mrs Latimer.'

Coffee finished; we went to our respective vehicles. 'You must be doing well to afford a Maserati,' I said, hoping I didn't sound rude.

'It's my brother's car,' he replied. 'He works overseas but he lends it to me occasionally. I borrowed it when I heard I was doing this trip. My own car's very boring.'

And he was gone.

I climbed back into Morag and put her in gear. There was a long road ahead.

Chapter 12

Night found me a bit further north than I'd expected. I'd stayed on the motorway at Glasgow and Stirling, only pulling in for a rest at Broxburn Services at Perth. I refilled Morag's thirsty innards with diesel then looked at the row of fast-food outlets for my supper.

Afterwards, I looked at the map and decided to go a bit further north. Before that, I rang Katie's number. It went straight to voicemail again, and I said – 'Hi, its Wendy. I know I said I'd be with you on Wednesday, but I'm going to stay at Aviemore tonight. It's taking longer than I thought. Call me when you get this? Bye.'

The A9 was confusing. From Stirling to Perth, it was dual carriageway all the way. It wasn't quite as scary as the motorways had been, and I'd made good time. I passed turn offs for places I'd like to have seen, like Gleneagles and Dunblane, and I wondered about the roads I'd take south. The route into Perth looked complicated and another motorhome driver in the Broxburn car park told me I'd be better off stopping closer to Inverness. North of Perth it wasn't dual carriageway all the way—there were bits of two-way road, punctuated by short stretches of dual carriageway

Malbister

when it seemed everything on the road passed Morag. At one point I was stuck behind a tractor for ten long miles. I pulled off at Pitlochry to get my bearings and went for a walk from the car park to the Festival Theatre, looking across at the river and the salmon ladder. The little town was touristy, with ice cream shops and gift shops all along the main street. I was enjoying the fresh air, when the phone beeped. A text from Katie

Soz – not convenient for u to visit. K x

I could have screamed. I'd blown my fuel budget, and spent three days on the road thinking she was in trouble. The least she could have done was ring me – not send a sodding text.

I replied. 'I'm on my own in Morag. I'm going to do the NC500 anyway now. I don't need u to put me up.'

I rang the number again and it went straight to voicemail once more. I left another message:

'Are you okay, Katie? I've come up this way because I'm worried. I really want to see you. I should be with you tomorrow afternoon. Bye.'

I wondered if anyone else had heard from her. I got on WhatsApp, using some of my precious data allowance and rang Dad. Give him his due, he picked up at the third ring.

'Katie? It's not the best time, pet. I'm out with a friend.'

Mum's best friend, of course. The one who was staying with him.

'I won't keep you long, Dad. Have you heard from Katie recently?'

A pause. 'Now you come to mention it, the last time she rang me was at Easter. I've been so busy lately, I hadn't noticed.'

Katie always rang home at least twice a week when Mum was alive. Dad was always happy to boast about her latest promotion or where she was going on holiday next. I used to think he did it to rub in the fact that I was a disappointment. But for Katie not to ring for over two months?

'Listen, Dad, I had a call from her – a weird one, and I've got a feeling there's something wrong. Every time I try to ring her, it goes to Voicemail and she sends texts. That's not like her, is it?'

'Maybe it's the phone reception up there in the Highlands? She did say the house is in the middle of nowhere.'

'Dad, has she asked you to visit at all?'

'Not so far, pet. But she did say that Malcolm has a lot on and they've work to do on the new house.'

He hadn't even asked how I was or where I was, for that matter. 'Dad, I've driven up to the Highlands in Morag. I'm planning on dropping in on her. I've come too far to turn back now, so if you know anything, now would be a good time to tell me?'

A female laugh trilled in the background. For someone who appeared broken hearted at the loss of his wife, Dad was playing the part of the merry widower rather too much for my liking. I wondered if he was planning a wedding of his own?

'I'm sorry, but I have to go. If she rings me, I'll let you know. Bye for now.' With that he hung up.

I made a point of booking into a decent campsite that night. The people I'd met in Perth services suggested Glenmore, and I'd rung ahead. Luckily, they'd had a cancellation and I managed to get a pitch with an electric hook up and water. I took my bag of washing into their laundrette and got talking to some younger campers who were on their way back from the NC500. They gushed over

Malbister

scenery and the folly of trying to drive over the twisty Bealach na Ba road at Applecross. I said I was going up the east coast and they gave me some suggestions for places to visit.

I mentioned I was headed for Malbister, which they didn't recognise, until I mentioned it was an estate, fairly close to Wick. One girl said they'd not bothered with Wick apart from driving through it on the road south. A couple who came in just after them said, 'Hey, Wick? Place with the shortest street in the world, and the first place to be bombed by the Nazis in the war. You don't know what you're missing.'

The girl said, 'You wouldn't happen to be from Wick, would you?'

He laughed at that and said, 'I'm biased – but don't write it off.'

I said I was on the road to visit a relative, but also that I was looking for a bit of casual work, 'Just a week working in a bar would help keep my van moving.'

He pulled out his phone and sent a text. 'If I hear of anywhere needing cover, I can ring you. What's your number?' I gave him my details and returned with my clean washing to Morag. At least, if I got turned away at the gates, I might make back the cost of the journey.

Chapter 13

June 6th

The next morning, I got up early, and was on the road and in Inverness by ten o' clock. I parked Morag in the theatre car park and went for a walk by the river.

I sent a text to Katie:

In Inverness. Will be near Wick late afternoon.

It was up to her now.

I needed to clear my head so I walked up to the castle and took in the view. I'd not been in Inverness for at least a decade and the place had grown arms and legs, spreading out in all directions. When Katie's first text had come, I'd hoped we might have met in this city, perhaps lunching in one of the nice restaurants near the bridge. I'd passed two and just reading the menu made me feel hungry – but I couldn't afford to waste money on a hasty meal for one.

Katie was always generous, and in the past if we dined out, she would insist on picking up the bill. She said she felt a bit guilty that while she had lots of expense account meals, that she didn't have to feed four people, or get two kids through school and college. She lived alone with two cats, and when she was at conferences, she had a sitter come in to live with them and she would phone home and ask to speak to them. She never forgot Christmas or birthdays, and Mum got flowers once a fortnight, on a subscription Katie set up. She gave Matt and Amy their first smart phones, and Matt's current laptop was a top of the range MacBook Pro that she had handed him when her company bought her a newer model. Amy's summer job was the result of her having a friend with useful contacts in France.

She'd done so well that Dad could boast about his clever and successful younger daughter, while putting down her sister and her family. Matt had a B.Sc. and an M.Sc., was starting a doctorate, but because he was Kevin's son, he barely registered on his grandfather's radar. This was the first summer Matt had taken off – every other summer, if he wasn't interning, he was labouring on the building sites. When I felt bad about it, he joked about it being cheaper than joining a gym, for building muscle tone.

Malcolm Goddard had three children, but so far, we'd not met any of them. I wondered how Katie felt about being a mum to a ready-made family?

I returned to Morag and set off on the last leg of the journey north. It was late morning and the sun was shining. Why, then, did I feel so anxious?

Chapter 14

Joe Ricci was right. Every second vehicle on the road was a campervan or motorhome. Most of them were coming in the opposite direction, but every layby had at least three vehicles closely parked together. At one point a huge motorhome, easily twice the size of Morag, was holding up a line of traffic behind, and a southbound ambulance lost patience and used blues and twos, to speed a patient to the hospital in Inverness. I didn't dare look at the scenery while I was driving, so I treated myself to a stop at Golspie beach. I'd looked on Joe's map and it looked as if the big attraction was the castle. I couldn't spare the cost of an entrance ticket, but I decided to go for a walk following the coastal path and get a glimpse of it from the shore. I peered through a gate straight out of Alice in Wonderland at gardens worthy of Versailles and above it to a fairy tale castle, with turrets and towers.

Katie loved fairy tales when we were growing up. An aunt gave us a beautifully illustrated book of Charles Perrault stories, and she would turn the pages with a sense of wonder than I couldn't quite understand. She loved Cinderella, and Puss in Boots and Sleeping Beauty. I was too much of a

Malbister

tomboy to like stories that began with Once upon a time and ended with everyone living happy ever after. Dunrobin was a perfect example of a Disneyesque castle, but my brochure told me it was built on heartbreak and blood. The English Duke of Sutherland fancied himself as an agricultural innovator and visionary, so he got his factor to throw the crofters off their land and put sheep on it. Like those peasants, I was at the gates, I was at the outside, looking in.

Well, Katie had her fairy tale, or so she thought. I just hoped it wasn't going horribly wrong.

When I got back to Morag, an old man, walking an arthritic border collie, gave me a filthy look. The car park was filled with tourists and camper vans, and it took all my concentration to reverse out and get back on the road.

As I drove north, the scenery changed. There was leafy woodland coming out of Golspie, but as I headed north of Brora, the trees became increasingly sparse, and the road through Helmsdale was scrubland and rugged coast. Kate had written about Berriedale in an email, shortly after she moved north, and I annoyed the drivers behind me by slowing down to tackle the Braes, holding my breath on the last hairpin bends, and praying that Morag's clutch would cope with the gradient. I was travelling through moorland now and passing small villages, each with its own harbour. There would be time to explore, I hoped, once I had seen Katie.

A week ago, I would have been terrified of the road north. A week ago, I was licking my wounds, packing up my life and mourning my failing marriage. I wondered where my new confidence stemmed from?

Malbister wasn't on any map. Katie's email had mentioned it being a few miles south of Wick, and I'd expected it to be another coastal village with its own tiny

Julie MP Adams

harbour. I'd stopped to ask for directions at the village shop in Lybster, and after some shaking of heads and suggestions of other places, they finally found someone to ask who could give me directions. It wasn't a village — but an estate. The local who set me on the right track was tight mouthed when I asked what sort of place it was and if he knew my sister. 'Incomers,' he said, 'Lots of money been spent on that place.'

And less an estate, than a fortress, I realised as I drew up at nine feet high wrought iron gates and pressed the intercom.

Chapter 15

The disembodied voice that responded to the buzzer was young, posh and male. 'Yes? What do you want?'

'I'm here to see Mrs Goddard. I'm her sister, Wendy Latimer,' I said, firmly.

'Do you have an appointment?' he asked.

'She knows I'm coming,' I replied. 'Can you get her for me?'

I waited outside those gates for quarter of an hour, when a Range Rover pulled up behind me and hooted loudly. A tall, lean woman with sharply bobbed steel grey hair and even sharper features got out and tapped a code into the key pad. The gates slowly opened and, back in her driver seat she hooted for me to proceed up the private road, with her following. In the mirror, I saw the gates swing shut behind her. I wondered who they were desperate to keep out, or keep in?

The ruined Malbister House – a Victorian hunting lodge, burned out and roofless, stood to the left, at the end of the road, but the new Malbister occupied a better position to the right of it, on an escarpment. It was a modern building, and bigger than the original had been, with two wings at right angles to the main structure. There were three enormous cathedral windows, a glass walkway around the upper floor and from what I could see, at least half the building was glass. I thought back to the grand designs Kevin had for the mill, and sighed. This place must cost a fortune. From any of those windows, you could see across peatlands and flow country to the sea.

The woman ignored me and strode into the house, slamming the door behind her. I got out of Morag, crunched my way across the driveway and pushed at the door, but found it locked and there was loud barking coming from inside.

I wondered how Katie's cats, Sauerkraut and Pickle felt about living with the two Weimaraner hounds that bared their teeth at me through the glass door?

Part of me wanted to go back into Morag, and cry with exhaustion and frustration, but the other part was ready for a fight.

Who were these people, and what had they done with my little sister? I looked around at the terrain: further down the hill was a stand of young pine trees, and what looked like some sort of ancient tower or broch. It looked bleak and inhospitable, as did the new house, but there was a fascination about the view. On a summer day with a deep blue sky, it was beautiful; in winter, it would be utterly bleak.

I pressed the doorbell, but became aware of pattering footsteps behind me. Two slender girls, in their mid-teens, dressed in ripped skinny jeans and broderie anglaise tops watched me. They had curling auburn hair, which fell to their shoulders and with their designer sunglasses, I couldn't read their expression.

Finally, one of them deigned to speak. 'Who are you and why is *that* in our driveway?' she pointed with utter disdain

Malbister

at Morag. I was itching to slap her, but at that moment, the front door swung open and my sister appeared. I was expecting a warm welcome and a hug, but to my horror, she shrank from me.

'Wendy? What are you doing here?' she said.

She knew perfectly well why I was here.

'Dad said you've not called him for two months. He's worried. I told him I was going on holiday in the Highlands and I said I'd look in on you,' I said. My fingers were crossed inside my back pocket. Technically it was the truth. She hadn't rung Dad. And I was supposed to be on holiday.

'It's not a good time,' she said. 'Malcolm has business guests staying, He's gone to the airport to fetch them.'

'It's fine,' I snapped. 'I've got my own accommodation. All I need is an outside tap and a place to empty my waste water tank. I've come to see you – not to sponge off you. Now, are you going to ask me in?'

Chapter 16

I didn't even get to set foot over the threshold of Malbister that first night. Perhaps it was just as well.

Instead, Katie told me to get back inside Morag and she climbed in and sat in the passenger seat beside me. 'Didn't you get my message, Wendy? This really isn't a good time.' She was obviously flustered.

I was furious. 'Do you know how far I've driven? I got that call and the message. Who was hurting you, Kate?' I pulled out my phone and played her the message. 'What's this about?'

She didn't answer at first. Instead, she sat still, unable to make eye contact, and I saw that she was changed. Her short hair had grown out to shoulder length, tied back, but it was lank, and without its usual sheen. She wore the uniform of the upper crust, Sloane Ranger wife – straight cut jeans, a Tattersall check shirt and a gilet, that were much too warm for a June day, even this far north, and her clothes looked two sizes too big for her. She wore no make-up, and her only jewellery was her wedding ring.

Malbister

'It was a mistake,' she said, at last. 'I'd had a bit too much to drink and we had a row.'

'Is he violent, Wendy? Was that the first time?'

She shook her head. 'He's got a bit of a temper, but it was my fault.'

'Oh, for goodness sake, Katie. What did Mum always say about men who hit women?'

There were tears on her cheeks and she sniffled, and scrabbled round for a tissue in the pockets of the gilet, finding one that was obviously well used. She blew her nose. I offered her another, from the packet in the dashboard, and she dabbed her cheeks and pulled down the mirror to check her face. Tears had dislodged the concealer she'd used to mitigate a bruise.

Whatever Kevin's faults, he would have slit his own throat before he would ever lift his hand to a woman. He might have been useless at business, but he stuck up for other people.

Someone let the dogs out into the grounds, and they came over to Morag and growled. Their cold grey eyes were disturbing and they ignored Katie's shout to them to sit.

'Are those your dogs?' I asked. 'How do the cats get on with them?'

'The dogs belong to Jack, my stepson. Malcolm has gun dogs, but they don't live in the house. And Sauerkraut and Pickle are in London with Betsy. Malcolm's daughters are allergic.'

'The girls I saw just now?' I asked.

She nodded.

Betsy, the cat sitter who used to stay over, adored the two ragdolls. They'd not suffer from lack of love—but the woman who sat beside me was another matter. She wasn't the Kate I knew.

'Please, Wendy. This really is the worst time. If Malcolm sees your van here when he gets back, he'll be furious.'

So, she was scared of him.

'Who's the woman with the hatchet face?' I asked. She'd looked vaguely familiar, and I was trying to remember where I'd seen her before.

'That's Judith,' she replied. 'Malcolm's mother.'

'How long are his guests staying?' I asked. 'I'll find a place to stop, but I'm not leaving the area until you and me have had a proper talk. Dad is worried about you and so am I.'

'Don't you need to get back to work?' she asked.

'I've been made redundant. I'm on a training course that starts in September, but I was supposed to be looking for temp work. Am I likely to find anything round here? You wouldn't have need of domestic staff?' I was being sarcastic, but she wasn't rising to the bait. Normally my sister would have been full of positive, useful suggestions, but everything I said was going in one ear and out the other without any of it registering.

She looked into the rear of the van. It had only struck her now – 'Where's Kevin?'

'Working. The lease on our rental is up, and he's living in on this job.' I wasn't going to fill her in on the saga of my marriage until we had time to talk properly.

She sat in the passenger seat while I turned Morag and returned to the gates, where she keyed in the code to let me out. Not a prisoner then, if she was allowed to open them. I headed back to the main road, and as I did so, a vast SUV with blacked out windows barged past me, almost putting me into the ditch. I had a glimpse of Malcolm Goddard in the driver's seat. I didn't see the passengers.

I drove back to the main road and headed into Wick. All the way since I passed Lybster, I was struck by how flat the

Malbister

countryside was: flow country, Joe's map called it. I passed a cemetery on the right, and a vast retail park on the left—the last thing you'd expect to find this far north. There were the usual No Overnight Parking signs, but two vans were parked up beside the graveyard. The main road passed side streets with trees, and a bowling green, with the local hospital, to my left and to my right I glimpsed that shortest street in the world: Ebenezer Street. I took a right turn and parked beside the river, walking back to get a photograph. I made it a selfie, and posted it on my Instagram page, and shared it with Amy and Matt. I walked along by the river, past the bridge and onto a waterfront where yachts and small vessels tied up alongside pontoons.

I needed time to think. I might as well do it here, in Caithness.

Chapter 17

The most northerly county in mainland Scotland has extraordinarily big skies. I discovered that evening just how big as I sat on the dunes of Reiss beach, a few miles out from Wick. I lay back and took in the three-hundred-and-sixty-degree horizon. It was a fortnight until the summer solstice and still light after ten.

Some young people – locals – gathered stones from the shingle beach in front of an impressive old castle, and lugged them to the sand to use as the base for a fire pit. They were busy cooking sausages over the fire, and getting stuck into a carry out of beer and cider. I'd seen them shopping in the big Tesco earlier on, working out which of them had ID and looked 18 to pay for the trolley load.

I'd also seen the Audi A1 with Kate's personal plate draw up. For a split second, I hoped she'd thought better of our conversation, and driven into town to try to find me, but instead the two girls I'd seen earlier got out, along with their driver, a young man I took to be Goddard junior. Katie loved that little car—I wondered how happy she was with it being purloined.

I walked the length of the beach. The sands were silvery

Malbister

white, and a handful of tourists, with their dogs were doing much the same, with a dalmatian and a dachshund scooting to and fore out into the waves, shaking themselves vigorously as they bounded up to their owners.

Earlier, I'd left Morag locked in the supermarket car park and gone for a walk up to John O Groats Wick airport, to look at the black helicopter on the tarmac. It was late evening, but a flight was expected from Aberdeen so I took a seat in the terminal and watched the plane land, and the passengers descend the steep steps and come inside the building to collect bags from the luggage carousel. It might be a modest size of airport, but there were families there to greet passengers with a hug before shepherding them into cars or taxis. All of them had a warmer welcome than I had after driving the length of the British Isles.

I was looking out at the tarmac, and at the helicopter when one of the despatchers came over to me. 'That's the last flight of 'e night, lass,' he said. 'Are ye lookin' for someone?'

'I'm just wondering about that helicopter. Someone local?'

He thought a minute. Security, I presumed, would stop him giving out details. 'Let's just say it's visitors to one of 'e big hooses. Came up from London and interrupted a scheduled flight earlier on.'

'Were they guests of Mr Goddard?' I decided to lay my cards on the table.

He clammed up completely. 'Are you a reporter? We're no allowed to give out that information.' he said. The shutters had come down, rather like the response I'd had earlier in Lybster. Whatever was going on at Malbister, it wasn't popular with the locals—but they were playing their cards very close to their chest.

Julie MP Adams

I'd politely asked directions and then walked back to Morag and drove her the short distance to Reiss beach, which ran below a golf course. Even late into the evening, there were golfers out, thwacking balls across the fairway.

The view was peaceful—I'd taken binoculars with me and after I'd walked the beach and sat in the dunes, I swung them from Ackergill Tower – the castle along the beach, to the white turrets of Keiss, across the bay. By half past ten, the sky was turning to dusk, and the main light now came from the teenagers' fire. I'd walked past and they said they'd only leave once the fire burned out. They'd be back next morning to return the stones to the shingle. The boy who I spoke to reminded me of Matt.

He assumed I was a tourist. I walked up to where motorhomes were parked cheek by jowl in the golf club car park, ignoring the No Overnight Parking signs.

Inside Morag, I checked my messages. I'd decided to make up the double bed, and I stretched out on it, luxuriating in the space and fell asleep, with the sound of the waves lapping on the shore, filling my dreams.

Chapter 18

June 7th

I woke to a bright, sunny morning, and dressed hastily in shorts and a t shirt, pulling flip flops out of a locker. It was only 6am and I wanted to make the most of the beach being quiet. I set off again, past where the youngsters' fire had burned to ashes, and set off, the dunes to my left to where a stream split the sands a mile up the beach. There was a rusted odd shaped piece of metal – part of an old boat, I guessed, and some driftwood. I bent and collected some razor clam shells and a bit of sea glass, putting them in the pocket of my shorts.

On my walk back, I was passed by two horses. Their riders were steering them into the shallow water, and they trotted through the waves before turning and cantering back on the firmer sand. As it got closer to eight, the beach became busy as other campervanners walked dogs and had a bit of exercise before the golf club opened and chased their vehicles away.

A woman in her sixties was gathering rubbish with a grabber and a bin bag. 'Want a hand with that?' I called and she accepted gratefully, handing me another bag.

'I do this twice a week,' she said. 'You wouldn't believe the amount of plastic that ends up on here.'

It took us the best part of an hour, and we filled both bin bags with assorted rubbish: water bottles; crisp packets; and disgustingly several soiled nappies. 'Why can't people take their rubbish home with them?' I asked.

'Tourists,' she shrugged. 'Matilda – that's her horses over there – had a devil of a job parking her horse box and getting her two out this morning, thanks to campervans. Those two need the sea water to help with injuries, and she has to bring them out before she goes to work.' I thought of Morag, and felt ashamed.

I apologised for being inconsiderate and she gave a half smile. 'The company that came up with the idea of doing the NC500 didn't bother to ask the locals for their opinion. It was all about filling the rooms in their posh hotels all year round, and supporting local hospitality businesses. Nobody realised the campervan rental companies in Inverness were going to take the route over. My friend Eilidh lives out west and she said the fools think the whole 500 miles is a one-way system.'

'Anyway,' she sighed, 'what was the big draw of doing the NC500 for you?'

'I'm not, actually,' I replied, 'I came north to see my sister, but it hasn't worked out. Her husband has business guests and they're too busy to see me, so I thought I'd hang about for a few days until I get a chance to speak to her.'

We were almost back at the golf club, and I asked about the castle at the end of the beach. 'Ackergill Tower? That's one of the oldest castles in Scotland. Up until this year, it was a hotel for a while. I had my retirement dinner there, a few years back. All sorts of folk used to come and stay there – if

Malbister

they had enough money. The NC500 didn't save it, mind. It's been sold to an American woman, so it's unlikely any of us will ever see inside it again.'

'I'm being rude. We've not been introduced.' She held out her hand 'Annie Swanson. I live in Ackergill – just beside the wee harbour over there.'

'Wendy Latimer, from Bath,' I replied. 'Nice to meet you.'

'Where did you say your sister lives? Would I know her?' I got the impression that Caithness might be a county where it would be almost impossible to go unnoticed, so I took my chance.

'My sister, Kate, is married to a man called Malcolm Goddard. They live in a place called Malbister?'

I'd expected her to clam up, but instead, she looked thoughtful. 'You wouldn't have a kettle in that van of yours?'

We sat drinking tea in the front seats, which I'd turned round to face into the van, and I'd hurriedly tidied my bed. Annie Swanson was a widow, and a retired civil servant. Her late husband worked at Dounreay, but was a Wicker through and through. She loved the county, but missed her grown up son, who worked as an engineer in Derby. 'He's on at me to move nearer, so I can see more of my grandchildren. They come up for summer holidays, and I go down to visit them at Christmas.' She was a talkative woman and I got the impression she was lonely and glad of an excuse for a bit of company.

She knew something about Malbister. 'It used to be part of the Falconbury Estate Trust—the old landowners got into bother with the tax people over death duties after the Second World War, and they sold it to Falconbury Investments. After the financial crisis, ten years or so ago, it was put on the market, but nobody wanted it, apart from folk who stayed at the Tower and went shooting on the land. Then a bunch of squatters moved into the old hunting lodge. There were all sorts going on in there. One of the outhouses was used as a cannabis farm, and they held raves. The police used to try and raid it, but the squatters were a fly bunch and they had someone tipping them off.'

'Anyway, a couple of years ago, there was a fire. The squatters had moved on, but someone must have got in and torched it. The old house is just an empty shell. Your brother-in-law came up to look at it, but decided he didn't want to bother with restoring the ruin. It's a listed building so he wasn't allowed to demolish it. Instead, he brought up an architect and they put up that monstrosity across from it. And then he moved his family and his business up from London.'

She finished her tea and set the mug in my small sink. 'Tell, me, lass, are you close to your sister?'

I nodded. 'I used to be. Since she married Malcolm Goddard, she's cut herself off from us. She met him just before our mum died.'

'He's not popular round here. Normally, we don't see much of the toffs, unless they show up for things like the Mey Games, hanging around Prince Charles. For a while there was an arts festival, they used to turn out for. The cinema up in Thurso gets those live screenings, and if it's opera, you tend to see the place filled with them. Goddard? He's not one of them – all noblesse oblige and throwing the odd crumb to the peasants. He behaves like he's on an island and all of us are invisible.'

'I wondered how he even knew about this place?' I said. 'It's not as if it's close to London.'

'Oh, that's easy—he used to work for Falconbury. He didn't bother coming up here before, mind. But he picked

Malbister

the land up cheap before it went to auction. It annoyed some folk around here, no end. There are the remains of an old broch on that patch of land and Falconbury planted some trees, as a tax dodge, on peatland. The University of the Highlands and Islands asked for permission to work on the broch and he told them where to go. He doesn't come into town here at all if he can avoid it either.'

No wonder the people I'd asked earlier were so dry with me. If I didn't already dislike Malcolm Goddard, I think I would now.

Chapter 19

Kate normally brought her boyfriends home to meet Mum and Dad. We'd seen all sorts of men come and go, from the lad she dated at school (skateboarder, into Coldplay), to two University flirtations – including a medical student (Asian, thoughtful and too busy for group dates) and a teacher training Maths post grad (geeky, bad breath). From the point she started work, and became a suit wearing young professional, they tended to be bankers and she waited until she was sure any man, she brought home wouldn't be patronising or annoy Dad. She never dated a builder, so he couldn't moan about 'bloody brickies.'

Some of her banker boyfriends drank too much. One of them did too much cocaine and got violent. Another was her boss, and she ended up leaving the company and missing out on a promotion I knew she really wanted.

She set up the dinner to introduce Malcolm Goddard to the family in a restaurant on Old Brompton Road, close to her flat. She sent four first class train tickets for Mum and Dad, Kevin and me. Mum was out of sorts—normally when they went up to see Kate at weekends, they would stay on her sofa bed, and she would go shopping with Kate the next

Malbister

day, while Dad would go to a football match. Instead, the four of us got on a train at six pm and would be on the half past eleven one home. By any standards it would be a long and tiring day for us all.

Kev grumbled at having to leave work early to shower and change and be in a taxi for the station for half five. I'd looked out his smart casuals—he only had one suit. I'd taken half a day's leave and spent the afternoon washing my hair and looking through my wardrobe for something appropriate to wear. Mum spent half the day in the hairdresser, and she and Dad wore their best going out clothes. Dad glowered across the first-class carriage table at Kev. My husband scrubbed up well, but to my father he would always be a bloody brickie. First class has food and drink included in the ticket, so we had a drink and some snacks. Mum took her time over her gin and tonic, and Dad made a fuss about the ice in his scotch. I'd ordered Prosecco and Kev, characteristically had a beer.

Kev is a big man – well over six feet, and I'd planned for him to sit across from me, but Dad plunked himself down across the table from him, then moaned about the lack of leg room for the whole of the journey. Mum was nervous, taking out her compact and checking her face in the mirror several times. Looking back, I realise her illness was already consuming her, and that evening of trying to smile brightly and be charming and sparkling must have been agony for her. In the end, after Reading, when the couple in a double seat across from us got out, Kevin and I made the excuse of giving them legroom and we sat there.

Kev's hair needed no product to make it stand up—it did so naturally. He took his blazer off and loosened the tie I'd insisted he wore. 'So, who's this bloke Katie's seeing? How posh this time?'

Julie MP Adams

I shrugged. 'She met him at a conference last month, and they've been seeing a fair bit of one another. He's something to do with a hedge fund, and I think he does stuff with the Tory Party.'

He snorted. 'That's all we bloody well need.'

Dad gave him an evil look. Dad's voted Tory all his life. Kevin's family are Labour Party members, and his uncle is a councillor. Not to mention that the people who conned Kev into buying that Mill were Tories.

It was fair to say the evening did not have the best start. At Paddington, we scrambled into a taxi, but should have taken the Tube. Every single traffic light was red and we reached the restaurant at half past eight. I'd sent a text to update Kate on where we were. She was at the door to greet us. Malcolm sat at the table, checking emails on his phone. He stood up when he saw us, shook hands with Dad and Kev and pecked Mum on the cheek.

I was busy keeping an eye on Mum, who looked strained, so my first impressions of Malcolm Goddard were perfunctory. He was tall, but not as tall as Kev, and while my husband is built like a rugby player, Goddard had the build of a man who plays polo. His silver-grey suit had the sheen of mohair and silk mix, and his shirt was fine cotton with lavender stripes. He wore a Tag Heuer watch and hammered silver cufflinks. His hair was fair, turning to grey at the sides, and clipped short, thinning on top.

We sat down and the waiter brought a bottle of champagne to the table, poured four glasses and after small talk about the weather and the cricket scores (he'd been briefed that Dad is a fervent cricket fan) we studied the menus.

I nudged Kevin under the table. He was glazing over, and I didn't want him nodding off over dinner.

Malbister

'So, Malcolm, Katie tells me you work in banking?' Dad said, as our starters arrived.

Goddard picked delicately with his fork at his Parma ham and melon. 'Yes, David—may I call you David? I work with what you might call a hedge fund. These are interesting times for the City. I believe you worked with money yourself?'

Flattery—Dad was a branch manager with Nat West. Kevin picked up his melon and ate it with his hands, much to Dad's disgust. Then he said, 'Hedge funds? Legalised gambling, isn't it? Shorting stock and making money out of other folks' misery? You lot stand to do well with Brexit, don't they?' I gave him a vicious kick under the table. I agreed with Kevin, but this was Katie's night and it was up to us to be civil to Goddard. After all, I consoled myself, her men seldom stayed long enough to count as a relationship. The chances were, we would never have to meet him again.

'You'll have to forgive my oaf of a son in law, Malcolm. Brickies aren't noted for their understanding of the finer things in life.' Dad's suit was too tight. He'd put on a stone since he retired, and the only exercise he got was walking his neighbour's poodle to the park and back. He was red in the face, which didn't bode well for Mum later on.

We'd ordered our main courses. Dad and Kev had beef fillet, while Mum asked for a small portion of carbonara and I'd stuck with salad. Malcolm had salmon with olive paste and green beans. The food was delicious, but I couldn't enjoy it. Malcolm Goddard gave measured responses to Mum and Dad's questions. Dad wasn't exactly asking what his intentions were towards his younger daughter, but Goddard was acting as if that was the agenda.

Yes, he'd gone to Eton, but he was a bursary boy whose mother was a music instructor there. He was close to his mother. His father died when he was twelve, of cancer.

How old was he? Fifty next year and eight years older than Katie.

Mum cleared her throat. 'Katie tells us you're a widower? And that you have family?'

He set his fork and knife down and took a drink from the water glass. 'My first wife died in a skiing accident on our tenth wedding anniversary. My son is twenty this year. My second wife left nine years ago. I've only recently completed the paperwork to have her declared legally dead. She suffered very badly with post-natal depression after our twin daughters were born, and was suicidal. We never found her body.'

He held out his hand to Katie, who put hers into his and they smiled at one another. 'I didn't think I could find happiness again, but meeting Kate has convinced me that it's possible.'

Give Kate her due, she looked well in the glow of the candle on the table. She'd found a man that Dad would approve of, and now she would have a ready-made family. A grown-up son and two daughters. Goddard was wealthy, and she wouldn't be spending months on end in our parents' spare room with two small children while her husband sold the roof over her head.

Goddard was fastidious and precise, but he wasn't namby pamby – as my father-in-law would call a man who didn't play rugby or like a pint in the pub with the lads. I got the feeling that he had himself on a tight rein and we were seeing an edited version of the real Malcolm Goddard. I wasn't sure I'd like what was below the surface.

Mum got up to go to the bathroom, and went pale as a sheet, swaying as if she was dizzy. I leapt to my feet to help her.

When we got there, she nipped into a cubicle and

Malbister

seconds later I heard retching.

'Are you alright, Mum?' I called.

The toilet flushed. Kate came into the bathroom. 'Is something wrong?' she asked. She wasn't smiling—she looked anxious and a little scared.

Mum emerged, wiping her mouth with the corner of the lace edged hanky she always kept in her bag. 'No need to fuss, dears. I must have drunk a bit too much.'

She insisted on our going back through, but asked me to bring her a glass of water. When I got back to the table, Dad and Malcolm appeared to be getting on well, while Kev had vanished through to the gents.

I delivered Mum's water to her and she produced some pills from her bag and put them in her mouth, swallowing them with a swig of water.

Kev emerged from the gents as we were coming out of the ladies. He took one look at Mum and got the waiter to order a taxi back to the station. I returned to the table and said that Mum wasn't well and we were going to take her home, but Dad should stay and get to know Malcolm, and catch up with Katie.

Thinking back, it was the wrong thing to do. I should have insisted on Mum staying over at Kate's flat. It turned out later that she'd already moved in with Malcolm, leaving her friend and cat sitter, Betsy to sub-let her place, and Mum would have needed to stay in an hotel. We got back to Paddington in time for the half ten train, and on the return journey she slumped in her seat, falling asleep and waking up with a start from time to time. Kevin almost carried her to the taxi at the other end, and we got her into her house and didn't leave until she was in bed asleep and Dad arrived home.

'Of all the rude things to do,' he growled at Kev. 'Ruining

Katie's evening...' He was just getting started and I didn't want him waking up Mum.

'Listen, Dad. I think Mum's ill. Has she seen a doctor?'

He looked at me blankly. 'I don't know. She might have.'

'Ask her tomorrow, and if she hasn't, I'll make an appointment for her. She was really sick tonight, and she's lost at least a stone. I'm worried about her.'

We finally got home where Amy was waiting up for us. 'Well,' she asked, 'Has Aunt Kate found her prince?'

Kevin snorted and went up to bed. 'To be honest, pet, I'm not sure about Aunt Kate's new man. I'm more concerned about your gran. She wasn't well tonight.'

Thinking back, I realise now why I gave up my brilliant career in London. Dad was a bully, and Malcolm Goddard was exactly the sort of man he'd approve of. I was always scared for Mum. Dad didn't deal out physical blows—he was much more subtle. It looked as if Katie had chosen a man like Daddy.

Chapter 20

I gave Annie Swanson a lift to the road end at Ackergill village, and drove back through Wick and back onto the south road. I intended to find somewhere to park Morag, and unhook my bike to do a bit of snooping round Malbister.

My phone rang just as I pulled into the retail park. I half hoped it would be Katie, ringing to arrange to meet me, but to my surprise it was Matt. 'Hi, love,' I said, 'How's the dig going?'

'It's not,' he replied. 'Politics stuff, but the upshot of it is, we're about to be deported. I asked if they could send me on to my next port of call, but the consulate says they have to send me home. Okay if I come home for a week or so—just until I can make travel plans? '

I hesitated. 'Didn't I mention we don't have a home right now? The landlord sold the house and your dad is living on site.'

'So where are you, Mum? I rang Dad and he said you'd run off with Morag. Said he'd been trying to email you, but you'd gone quiet on him.'

I'd blocked Kevin on my email, in a fit of rage after he announced he was working for that woman. I felt guilty—I was relying on keeping direct contact with my kids, but forgetting that they have two parents and not every conversation included me.

'Well,' I began. 'Your aunt lives in the Highlands and I thought I'd take Morag on the NC500.'

He laughed. 'You and the rest of the world. How come you got over your fear of motorways to drive a thousand miles? How's Aunty K?'

'I'm not a complete coward, Matthew Latimer. She's too busy to see me. I'm hanging around Caithness until her visitors leave.'

I heard a muttered conversation on the other end of the line. 'Mum, what's the name of that place she lives in? '

'It's Malbister,' I said. 'Near Wick.'

There were voices on the other end. He was speaking to someone else. 'Are you still there?' I asked.

'Hey, Mum. You didn't notice a round tower sort of thing near the house? Something called a broch?'

I assented.

'They're ancient structures. One of the team here is from Orkney and she says it would be cool if we could get a look at it? I can ask to get flown home and bus it up to you, if that's okay?'

'Are you sure?' I asked. 'Wouldn't it be uncool to be around your old mum?'

'I've to deliver a paper on geology and ancient sites. I've got enough for the work here, but that broch at Malbister could be what I'm looking for. Don't worry—Freya and me will have our camping gear with us. Just don't go doing a disappearing act before I get to you.

Chapter 21

To be honest, I had mixed feelings about my son and Freya appearing in Caithness. On the one hand, I'm always glad to see my boy, but it was proving tricky enough to get to see Kate by myself. Having a geologist and an archaeologist trying to research on Malcolm Goddard's land, after a university had tried and failed, might not be the wisest thing we could do.

On the other hand, Freya was from Stromness, and they could very well just be passing through on their way to get a few days at her family home before setting off on their next adventure. I'd held back some money in case he needed it. The weather would need to be good enough for wild camping for a night or two. I doubted he would want the over cab bunk.

What it had shown me, though, was my plan to keep moving over the summer had a flaw. Kevin might have let me down, but the kids both love him, and it wasn't fair to drive a wedge between them. So, I checked my emails and unblocked him.

June 6th 'Where are you, Wendy? I'm worried about you. Call me – love Kev.'

Julie MP Adams

June 5th *'Wendy, what are you thinking of? I rang Dorothy and she said you were travelling in Morag. Please be really careful.'*

June 3rd *'Wendy, whatever you think is going on between me and Mrs C – it's not. Okay? Call me.'*

I replied *'It's me, Wendy. I'm in Caithness, trying to visit Katie. Matt is back in UK and heading up to join me. I'm fine and I'm taking care. NC 500 is very, very busy. We need to talk when I get back.'*

I checked what I'd written, then reluctantly added, *'How is the job going?'*

I pressed send. There. Now he knew where I was.

I found a parking space out of town, a few miles from Malbister and unhooked my bike from the back of Morag. I wanted to check out the countryside around the Goddard place and I could make the excuse I was doing touristy things. Annie Swanson gave me a list of several places I needed to visit, and one of those, the Whaligoe Steps, was fairly near to where I was parked. It had been ages since I'd ridden my bike. I strapped on my helmet and checked the tyres and brakes. I annoyed drivers going south. There didn't seem to be any dedicated cycle paths.

Whaligoe is a tiny inlet harbour at the foot of a narrow, spiral steps. There's a step for every day of the year, but I stopped counting after two hundred, focussing all my attention on not losing my footing. There was what looked like a nice café in a substantial square-built stone house at the top of the steps and I promised myself a hot drink on my return climb. I'd noticed two other bikes when I leaned mine against the wall and fastened my padlock, but I'd assumed their owners would be in the café. As I neared the bottom of the steps, I saw two copper-coloured heads and realised it was the Goddard twins. They were sitting with their legs dangling over water that was so deep it was almost black.

I wasn't sure if they'd recognised me, and looking at

Malbister

them from above, I could tell they were conspiring against someone or something. As I approached, they looked up, and their faces hardened. They pushed past me and ascended the steps two at a time. I had the place to myself for a moment, and I sat and took in the almost claustrophobic atmosphere of the tiny cove. I tried to imagine the fisherwomen climbing those steps with heavy creels strapped to their back, filled with herring.

I'd asked Kate, before the wedding, about her new ready-made family. The twins were to be her bridesmaids, and they'd had dress fittings.

We'd always promised that when she finally got married, I was to be her matron of honour. Years ago, we'd laughed over how matronly my dress would actually be. Kate had chosen her ideal wedding dress—it would be demure at the front, with a low cowl back, sleeveless, low waisted and ivory velvet. By chance, she sourced the exact dress, but had puzzled over the bridesmaid frocks. I'm blonde and the twins with their red hair would make a choice of colour tricky.

After Mum's diagnosis, she brought the wedding forward, but couldn't find the right venue. Malcolm Goddard suggested a friend's hotel in the Maldives, and would fly Mum and Dad over, but drew the line at the rest of the family. He thoughtfully said he was thinking about the strain on my mother.

Little by little, Katie's wedding plans were rubbed away. Malcolm didn't think her choice of dress was appropriate for a woman over 35, so her dream dress gave way to an Anna Valentine cream shantung silk shift with a matching coat. In place of a tiara and veil, she wore a fascinator. It looked matronly and more like the mother of the bride than a bride, when she tried it on before they set off for the Maldives, I told her so. Her ring might be a five-carat oval diamond from Tiffany, but she'd been short changed.

What was behind the choice? The twins didn't want to wear frilly frocks. They turned up to the wedding in their ripped jeans, which upset Mum no end.

The girls were a stubborn pair, closely bonded and in the absence of their birth mother, raised by Malcolm's mother, Judith and a succession of nannies who tended to walk out over their behaviour. By the time of the wedding, they were at a prep school, and this year would be starting at Fettes College, which their older brother had also attended.

I wondered how they would react to wearing school uniform, but Kate reckoned school was the only place they seemed willing to conform.

The wedding was miserable, she told me. 'I wanted my big sister there. I wanted Mum to be well. The ceremony was in a hotel dining room, because it was October and it rained solidly. But Malcolm seemed happy and Dad was sucking up to him like mad. I felt sorry for Mum.'

Only in the past twenty-four hours had I set eyes on the twins. I didn't even remember their names, although Kate had told me. Their defining feature was their hostility. I'd now seen them several times and they had done little to endear themselves.

I remained at the cove for half an hour before making my way up the steps, leaning to one side to let other people descend. At the top, I checked my bike before getting my coffee. Both tyres were flat, possibly because there were slashes in both. The twins really didn't like their stepmother's sister.

I took my time over the coffee, checking to find out if my bike could be repaired, or if I'd need to wheel it back to Morag. The problem was solved when I realised across the

Malbister

café, at a seat beside a vast picture window, sat Joe Ricci.

He looked up from the local paper he was reading, and flashed a smile of recognition. 'Mrs Latimer! We meet again.'

'There wouldn't be any adverts for a bike repair shop round here in that paper?'

'I shall check, dear lady.'

I nipped across to sit at the same table. 'You didn't happen to see two young girls, did you? Auburn hair? About five foot eight?'

He nodded.

'I think they slashed my bike tyres.'

'They wouldn't happen to be April and Augusta Goddard by any chance?' He sighed and put the paper down.

'You know them?' he certainly seemed to get around. And he seemed very knowledgeable.

He finished his coffee and took a bite from a pastry, before answering. 'I know of them. You didn't say you knew Goddard?' He looked wary—something I'd not noticed in him before. Then he said – 'Oh. The hedge fund manager brother-in-law?'

'Yes. I've tried to catch up with my sister and it seems the house is like a fortress and she can't get out to see me because they have visitors.' There. My cards were on the table. 'I worry about her.'

'That'll be Shaikh and his sons. Goddard does a lot of business in the Middle East. I'm sorry, Mrs Latimer. You have my sympathies.'

'You said you knew of the twins?' I asked.

He called across for two more coffees and a glass of water. When they arrived, he added a spoon of sugar to his cup and stirred it. I took a sip of mine, and prompted, 'Well?'

He looked out the window at where two more tourists were descending the steps. 'I knew the second Mrs Goddard

— the twins' mother. Maria worked in sales for the same design company as me. Lovely woman, a real beauty, but didn't seem to know the effect she had on men. When she was working on a project overseas, about fifteen years ago, she was assaulted, and it knocked her confidence for six. She became very fearful and nervous – not like her at all.'

'She was Italian, like me, but from Venice. She was working for her family business in a ski resort. She met Goddard there. It was a year after his first wife died in a skiing accident. It was much too soon for either of them. He was a widower with a ten-year-old son, and she was very fragile.

'Somehow, he convinced her that she wanted to be looked after, and he married her within a few months. He talked her family out of a big church wedding, and then it was as if she just vanished. The last I'd heard was that she had twin daughters and that she was being treated for depression. That didn't surprise me, after what happened to her before.'

He frowned.

I took up the thread. 'Kate met Malcolm Goddard at a conference. He told her his second wife was being declared legally dead. That she vanished when the babies were only months old?'

The café owner was bustling around with a cleaning spray and a cloth, clearing tables and setting up for lunch. She smiled at us 'No, you're fine. We've got lunch bookings for noon. You've a while yet.'

'Goddard said she vanished in the middle of the night when he was away on business. He told the police she was disturbed,' Joe said.

'Do you think she's dead?' I asked.

He shrugged. 'It wouldn't be like Maria to leave her

Malbister

children. Family meant the world to her. But if she disappeared, I wouldn't trust Goddard not to have had something to do with it.'

Chapter 22

Joe drove me back to where Morag was parked and I drove back to Whaligoe to collect the bike and put it on the rack. It turned out there was a bike shop in Wick, so by mid-afternoon, I had two new bike tyres. I also had a temporary job. Joe was holding meetings across the North Highlands to promote his flat pack holiday home plans, and he wanted an assistant to meet and greet, hand out brochures and take names of interested parties at five meetings held in hotels around the route of the NC500.

The first meeting was tonight, at the Norseman Hotel by the riverside, where he was staying. I'd had the presence of mind to take a couple of smart frocks with me, and a pair of heels. Even better, he let me use his room to get changed and have a shower before the meeting. Applying my mascara and running straighteners through my hair, I began to feel like my former self.

We had a bar supper before the event, and he explained: 'I'm trying to convince some landowners that diversification is going to be necessary. Right now, there's a lot of land devoted to sheep farming, but the market for lamb tends to be Europe, and if the likes of your brother-in-law get their

Malbister

way, there's going to be a No Deal Brexit and lots of farmers will really struggle to make ends meet. On the other hand, the NC500 is pulling tourists into the area, and lots of them are in motorhomes or campers. One solution is for farmers to set aside a field for 'aires' – places where you can empty grey water tanks and chemical toilets, and park up for the night. Add a laundrette and a café, and that's a new income stream that could keep people on the land. But create a glamping pod park, with hot tubs, and fire pits, you expand the hotel capacity. My plans are to stop houses that key workers need being bought up by Londoners as holiday lets.' He handed me a brochure. 'I want you to spend a while looking at this, so you can answer questions.'

Joe's company produced a type of tiny house, off grid and self-sufficient, with rainwater tanks, composting toilets and solar panels. Because they were built on something like a lorry trailer, they were less of a headache for planning permission. 'If it all goes wrong, they can move the lodges to another site, or sell them on. I've seen people take up the option of glamping pods and get mired in lots of red tape, because those need to be plumbed into septic tanks and you need planning permission to site them. The idea behind this is that anyone with a decent sized garden can stick a couple of these into their space under permitted development, and they can be leased out as Air B n B or longer term to people who want a holiday in the North Highlands every year, say for a month at a time – or maybe for the whole summer. They aren't static caravans per se, but they come under similar regulations.

'My biggest obstacle,' he said, taking a drink from his non-alcoholic beer, 'is the major landowners who would rather do another Highland Clearance and turn everything into deer park for stalking. Some of them own too much of the land and they don't want anything to change. Your brother-in-law, for instance, doesn't want campers on his land, and I doubt he'd be happy if his neighbours wanted to diversify.'

The brochure showed what looked like a simple cabin. The interior designs put Morag to shame, with a proper kitchen and bathroom and a sleeping loft, and an L shaped sofa bed. I thought Kevin and I could live in that full time.

'Who's making them for you?' I asked.

'So far, there are only two prototypes, and they're being made in a shed in the West Country, by a few guys who came to the first meeting. '

We had the hotel lounge for the meeting, and I was stationed at the door with a table, a pile of brochures and a clipboard to gather names and details of people who might be interested.

I'd welcomed my twentieth customer, and was about to assume my second task inside the meeting, handing out refreshments, when I looked up into the cold grey eyes of Malcolm Goddard's son, Jack. His grandmother strode straight into the lounge and took a place at the back. He walked past me without acknowledging my presence. I wrote their names on the sheet of paper, then got up, went inside and closed the door.

Joe had a screen and a projector ready and it was down to me to hand out brochures and refreshments. Jack and Judith Goddard took brochures without a word of thanks and declined the glasses of Prosecco.

There was a buzz in the room, as most of the people there became aware of who was sitting behind them.

Joe took up position and welcomed everyone to the presentation. Then he launched into the sales pitch. He was good—I grant him that—but when he came to the Q and A

Malbister

part of the evening, Judith Goddard stood up. 'What you propose is an abomination. My son has a controlling voice in four estates in Caithness, and I assure you that you will find opposition if you try to put these.... huts onto any land that is leased from these. She glowered round the room. I could swear she was taking a mental snap of every face in the room. Goddard had his phone out and was obviously filming. 'I assure you that you will have the same response elsewhere in Highland.'

She remained in her seat for the rest of the evening, scowling at the people who sidled up to Joe. The retired teacher, who had taken a brochure and talked about how this would help her pension, looked nervously across at her. 'My garden is right next to one of their estates. The last time I did something they didn't like; they took my dog and didn't give her back until I'd changed it back. I'm sorry,' and she handed the brochure back.

Two crofters handed theirs back too, muttering about the terms of their leases. As each person left the room, the two Goddards glowered at them. Finally, when there were only four of us in the room, Judith turned her attention on us. 'Mr Ricci, if you have any idea of what is good for you, you will leave now and forget any plans to sell your huts in this area. And as for you, Mrs Latimer—I'd be obliged if you would leave now. Your sister wants nothing to do with you – or the rest of your family.'

When we packed up, the hotel manager was apologetic, but nervous. 'We don't want any trouble, sir, but Mrs Goddard wants to cancel your booking for Thurso tomorrow and for Tongue the day after. '

Joe's expression hardened. 'My company paid for my bookings in full. I'm not cancelling. Mrs Goddard doesn't own your hotels, and therefore she cannot cancel without my consent. Cancel tomorrow and you'll be hearing from my solicitors.'

He looked at me, 'Wendy, are you okay?'

I wasn't. I put my hand up to my face and realised I was crying. Joe sat me down in the empty lounge and handed me a drink. 'I'm sorry,' gasped out between sobs. 'I'm just scared for my sister. God knows how she must feel being shut in with those people.'

Chapter 23

June 8th

The next day, I took the scenic route to Thurso, driving past Reiss and taking a right turn towards John O Groats. The land was flat with a long straight road through the village of Keiss, which eventually took me past several more ancient castles and into the place that is the nominal north point of mainland Britain. To the left, as I drove into Groats, were luxury versions of Joe's small houses, which I gathered cost a lot to hire in high season. The old hotel was painted in primary colours, and against an azure sky looked cheerful and bright. I took a selfie (for the benefit of Matt and Amy) at the signpost, and wandered around the visitor centre, buying a huge ice cream at Flavours, and savouring it in the sunshine.

I walked over to Duncansby Head and crawled on my belly close to the edge of the cliffs to see the puffins, whirring like tiny colourful helicopters. I had clumps of bog cotton clinging to my t shirt as I stood up.

The girl who served me in Flavours told me that the real north point was at the lighthouse at Dunnet Head, so I took

Julie MP Adams

Morag there, and got out to stretch my legs. I spotted Joe's flashy car parked further along, but didn't see him during my walk. The lighthouse at Dunnet is tall, white and according to Annie Swanson used to contain a recording studio. It has no shops, but these days has holiday lets. Joe said last night it was a potential site for his project, so I assumed he was inside the main building or meeting someone nearby. I sat in Morag, with my side door open, drinking a cup of tea and eating a sandwich, watching people coming and going. By the time it got close to four o clock I needed to start on the road, but there was still no sign of Joe. The Maserati drew the attention of the tourists. I dug in my glove compartment for the card he gave me and sent a text. 'In car park at Dunnet Head Lighthouse. Can see your car. Where are you? WL.'

No reply. I set off on the road, and drove through the village of Dunnet and out onto the road through Castletown, passing Murkle Bay and reaching Thurso shortly before 6pm. I tried ringing Joe's number when I parked Morag near the station and it went straight to voicemail. I was getting worried now.

I closed the blinds and got myself ready for the evening's presentation, scooshing dry shampoo into my hair and backcombing, before doing a strip wash and rinse in the tiny shower cabin, and struggling into my dress and heels. I walked down the road to the Pentland Hotel and asked if Joe had arrived to set up.

The receptionist looked at me blankly.

'Mr Ricci?' I repeated.

She checked her computer and shook her head. 'Mrs Goddard rang to cancel his room and the meeting room last night.'

I sat on a deep, comfortable chair at reception and

Malbister

checked my phone. There was no reply to my text and no missed calls. I'd have expected Joe Ricci to be here and making a fuss. Something wasn't adding up. I decided to stay around and wait to see if he turned up. I ordered a tonic water and a bag of crisps and constantly looked up to check as people came through the revolving door.

By half past eight there was still no sign of him. I'd sent more texts and tried phoning again, but there was no response. Aside from the car in the lighthouse car park, it was as if he'd vanished off the face of the earth.

I wondered why I felt so uneasy. It wasn't as if I really knew the man, anyway, apart from a few meetings over the past few days. However, Mrs Goddard's glare directed at him told me that we were allies in something, and I wasn't about to give up now.

Chapter 24

I returned to Morag and changed my heels for flat pumps. Although it was summer, it was chilly in the evenings and I pulled a pashmina from the locker and threw it over my shoulders. I walked down Princes Street, stopping into a chip shop to buy my supper and ate as I walked to the shore. There was a small beach and esplanade, and a man was walking two black Labradors, throwing a toy for them to chase. He shouted at another man in shorts who was running past me, and made the motion of drinking. The runner shouted back 'See you in the Comm in an hour!'

I liked the idea of life going on as normal. From what I could see, Thurso was like small towns all over the world. Annie said that before the 1950's, it was a smaller place, and just about everything built since then was down to a nuclear power plant at Dounreay bringing people up to live and work there. The nucleus of the town, like Wick, was old, with solid Georgian and Victorian buildings, but there were large housing estates and a secondary school designed by Sir Basil Spence, the architect of Coventry Cathedral, which I'd passed on my way down the hill. I passed a caravan site. I was fast running out of clean laundry, and I'd need to book

Malbister

into a site soon. Apart from washing, I needed to charge my laptop and catch up on what was happening in the outside world.

Where was Joe? I resolved to check to see if his car was still at the lighthouse tomorrow. I was more worried about Katie, to be honest. A week ago, I was concerned for myself, packing up my life and trying to fathom out what to do about my failing marriage. Suddenly I missed Kevin and the kids so much it hurt. Maybe the point of a road trip is to convince you there's no place like home, like it says in the Wizard of Oz.

As I reached Morag, I noticed a police car parked across the road. The young woman in the oversized padded high viz gilet emerged and crossed the road. 'You do know there's no overnight parking here?'

I nodded. 'I'm going to try and book into the caravan site.'

Then it struck me. 'Excuse me officer, but I was supposed to be meeting my boss for a presentation at the Pentland Hotel earlier this evening. He didn't arrive, and someone cancelled our event.'

She spoke into her radio and then I got her attention back. 'The thing is, I saw his car parked at Dunnet Head lighthouse earlier, but there was no sign of him, and he's not been answering his phone.'

She had her notebook out now and a pen. 'Go on?'

'Last night, our meeting had someone there that was trying to intimidate us. A Mrs Judith Goddard from Malbister Estate?'

She beckoned the other officer in the car to come over. 'Hey, Ally, you're from the Wick side. What do you know of Malbister?'

He frowned. 'Can't say, really, apart from them being

incomers.'

I added, 'My sister is married to Judith Goddard's son, and they've not let me see her. I'm concerned for her as well as for my boss.'

Ally Sinclair was tall, skinny and had a Prince William haircut to minimise his receding hairline. He used his radio to tell his HQ they were going to check out a possible abandoned vehicle at Dunnet. Then they sped off in their marked Volvo V70. I got the feeling that they were bored and this was giving them an excuse for a drive. I just hoped that Joe, wherever he was, wasn't in any sort of trouble.

Chapter 25

I managed to get the last site with an electric hook up at the caravan site, and spent the rest of the evening in the laundrette, doing my washing. Morag has two solar panels on the roof, but I wanted to recharge my phone and iPad properly, and it was a chance to try and do normal stuff like watching television. I found myself unable to concentrate, though, thinking of what might have happened to Joe. Judith Goddard was an absolute hard-faced cow, and I wondered how she treated Katie.

I didn't need to wait long to find out. The patrol car had noted down my vehicle registration and I'd given them my mobile phone number. Shortly before midnight, I saw their distinctive livery parking up at the main block, and soon after there was a tap at my door.

'Mrs Latimer? Would you mind answering some questions, please?'

I asked them into Morag, and apologised for the tight space. They sat in the driver and passenger seats, swivelled to face into the van, while I sat cross legged on my bed.

'Can you tell us how you came to meet Mr Ricci?' the female officer asked.

'I met him on the road, shortly after I started my journey north,' I replied. 'He was interested in my motorhome, because he used to work for the company that made her. I saw him again at a couple of points further north. I thought it was a coincidence.'

Ally Sinclair was writing in his notebook. They exchanged a glance. I wasn't reassured.

'And you say you were working for Mr Ricci?' she continued.

'He told me he needed someone to do meet and greet and hand out sales brochures,' I said. 'I was made redundant last week and I was planning to try and find temp work until my post grad course starts in September.'

'So, you thought you'd do the NC500?' Ally asked, looking up from the notebook.

'Not at first,' I replied. 'My lease expired and my husband's working away. I had a call from my sister. It sounded as if she was in distress and I decided to visit her. Her husband and his mother won't let her see me.'

It sounded horribly implausible, even to me.

'We had a report of the Maserati being stolen by a Mr Richards,' the female officer said. 'We also did a search on Giuseppe Ricci, and he has a criminal record. Is there any possibility that he might have been following you to try to get to Mr Goddard and his family?'

I shook my head. 'I only got the call from Katie after I started driving north.'

Ally Sinclair said, 'The thing is, Mrs Goddard has gone missing. Her husband was convinced she is with you.'

I shrugged. 'I wish. I've hardly had a moment to speak to her. What do you think has happened to her?'

Chapter 26

June 9th

I spent a miserable night, tossing and turning, and feeling like an utter fool. At three in the morning, I gave up trying to sleep and got up to walk along the shore. I stood on the harbour walls, looking across to the partially ruined Thurso East castle as the sun rose. The two police officers last night convinced me I'd been duped into some sort of plan to kidnap my sister. The Maserati was dumped in an obvious place and Joe Ricci had either kidnapped my sister or run off with her.

I'd sent text after text to Katie's phone:
Why didn't you trust me, Katie? Call me – W x
Are you safe? Just let me know where u are? W x
This isn't funny, sis. I'm scared. W x

I returned to Morag worn out and fell into an exhausted doze, waking up after eight am and feeling like death warmed up.

Finally, this morning I'd tried calling. The call was picked up on the third ring, but not by Katie. 'Who is this?' a male voice said. It sounded as tired as I felt.

'It's Wendy Latimer. I want to speak to my sister,' I snapped.

'As do I,' he snapped back. 'I thought she might be with you.'

'I saw her for exactly five minutes a couple of days ago, and your mother warned me off.' I thought for a moment. 'Why have you got her phone?'

There was a short silence. 'I found the phone in my daughters' room. They'd taken it.'

That explained the strange texts. His voice sounded less authoritarian, and more like a human being. 'Could I ask you to come here? I think we need to talk.'

So, he wanted to talk, now, did he? I'd been menaced by dogs; had my bike vandalised by his daughters and was intimidated by his mother. I didn't exactly look forward to a visit to Malbister. The thought of driving back through those gates was the last thing I wanted. The entire family were hostile, and I didn't want to face them on my own.

There was a beep. My phone had a WhatsApp message. I took a quick look. 'Hi Mum. I'm in Thurso. Where are you parked?'

I messaged my location. At least with Matt and Freya, I'd have allies. And Matt did say he wanted a look at that broch.

I returned to the call. 'Okay, but I've got my son and his girlfriend with me. I'm bringing them too.'

Matt and Freya clambered on board Morag, laden with heavy rucksacks. They looked tired and in need of a good wash and a meal. I hugged my son as if my life depended on it, and stood back to look at him properly. Then I got a whiff of stale body odour and he laughed. They fetched toiletries and a change of clothing from their luggage and I handed them my two clean bath towels. They disappeared off into the shower block and returned looking clean and tanned and

Malbister

disgustingly young and healthy. They'd been flown into London and spent the past day and a half on coaches.

Freya intended to catch the ferry home from Scrabster today, but hearing about a chance to see the broch, she agreed to come with us.

I took them to lunch in the Blue Door Diner on the campsite, and while ordering what Matt afterwards declared to be the best burgers and shakes, he'd ever tasted, I rebooked my pitch for later that night, which would give me an excuse not to get stuck on Goddard territory. There was too much to catch up over lunch, and I suspected we'd be talking long into the night.

We set off around midday, and this time took the straight road that bisected the county, and went through the village of Watten. We drove Morag through Wick, and arrived at the gates of Malbister as rain clouds swallowed the sun. Freya got out and pressed the intercom button, and the gates swung open to admit us.

My heart pounded as we walked together up to those huge glass doors. Matt made a joke about industrial supplies of Windowlene, which thankfully let me catch my breath. I could hear the dogs barking, but they were silenced as the door swung open and we were greeted by the cold stare of Malcolm Goddard.

Chapter 27

He showed us through into a room with a giant cathedral window. From where we sat on an oversized sofa, we could see over the landscape to the sea, several miles away. Matt got up and walked to the window, to look at the broch. I know how my son's mind works. Never mind aunt Kate— there was something about the structure that was preoccupying him.

Goddard got straight to the point. 'Where is my wife?'

'I don't know. Where is my sister?' I retorted. 'Why was her smartphone in your daughters' room?'

He looked older. He'd had a much shorter haircut, and most of it was more grey than fair now. His face was pallid, and he looked as if he'd not slept.

'How long has she been missing?' I demanded. 'And who was the last person to see her?'

I remembered what he told us about his second wife's disappearance, while the balance of her mind was upset. I remembered also what Joe Ricci said about her—that to walk out and leave her children was completely out of character. How well did I know Katie these days?

The girls entered the room and sat on the sofa opposite,

Malbister

while Judith Goddard stood behind her son, her sharp features cast into shadow.

'The morning of June 7th, I woke up, and she was gone. That wasn't unusual, because she usually goes running before breakfast, but she hadn't returned by lunchtime,' he said. 'I sent Jack out to look for her, because I had to entertain our guests, and because with clay pigeon shooting going on, I didn't want to risk her getting in the line of fire. He combed the estate with a fine toothcomb, but couldn't see her.'

I looked at Judith Goddard. 'The same day you told me my sister wanted nothing to do with me or the rest of my family? Odd, don't you think? Given that when I did speak to her the day before, I could see she was scared of you.'

Matt came back from the window and sat beside me. His quiet presence gave me courage. 'If anything has happened to Kate, I will never forgive you,' I told them.

Judith Goddard was looking at us through narrowed eyes. 'The man you were with is no friend to this family.'

Matt looked at me, eyebrows raised. 'I wasn't *with* Joe Ricci—I was doing some work for his company,' I explained. 'You seemed determined to throw a spanner in the works. And he's vanished too.'

'Rather convenient,' she snarled.

The girls, who had been unable to take their eyes off my handsome son, chose to act like perfect little angels and offered us tea, trotting off and returning with a butler and a tea trolley, laden with sandwiches and cake. Through a mouthful of scone, Matt commented, 'Aunt Kate is her own person. If she's left of her own accord, that's her decision and I'd support her in that. But you look the sort of man who has enemies, and if she's got caught up in crossfire, we won't forgive you if anything's happened to her.

'Besides,' he said, 'To paraphrase Oscar Wilde, 'to lose

Julie MP Adams

one wife is unfortunate, to lose two looks like carelessness – and three? Mr Goddard – there's no way on earth I'm calling you Uncle Malcolm—you seem to make a habit of this.'

Chapter 28

I thought back to the internet research I did on Malcolm Goddard, shortly after that awful dinner. Mum was my first priority at the time, and I didn't want her upset, but I'd rung Kate and forced her to have lunch with me the following Saturday. I didn't like him one little bit, and I tried to persuade her to take things slowly.

This morning, I'd got a more recent biography of Malcolm Goddard from a business journal online. It was an authorised and probably sanitised version. His father was a housemaster at Eton, and much older than Judith. He died of cancer when Malcolm was a boy and already had his scholarship place at the school, and while the headmaster was all too willing to throw the widow out of her accommodation, Judith applied for a job as a music instructor, and was housed in a single room in the school. She remained in post throughout her son's school years and during his time at Oxford and at Harvard Business School. He was a bright lad and graduated with a first in Economics, and by all accounts made some extremely lucrative contacts.

He met his first wife, Lady Fiona Smythe-Hamilton at Oxford, and they married in 1992, at the chapel of her family's estate in Hertfordshire. Jack was born in 1996, after Fiona miscarried a daughter. There were numerous pictures of the first wife, taken from the society pages of Hello and Harpers. Some showed her in the company of Diana and Fergie, both of whom she appeared to know well. She moved in similar circles – Ascot, polo matches, and skiing, and it was at Klosters – a society favourite resort – that another skier crashed into her, and she died from a brain injury on her way to hospital.

Goddard was doing well for himself by 2006, with Falconbury Investments hiring him as a fund manager. The family lived in a large apartment in Belsize Park, and Judith moved back in after Fiona's death, to help with Jack, who was inconsolable at the loss of his mother. She gave music lessons from the home and acted as housekeeper and nanny.

However, at the end of 2006, within ten months of the tragedy, Malcolm joined a group of business associates who planned a skiing holiday and had a spare ticket. It was there that he met Maria Gambini, and within a few months, married her. She was already pregnant with the twins at their wedding.

Maria was beautiful, talented, clever, and according to Joe Ricci, who claimed to know her, she was also vulnerable. When the twins were born in 2007, she suffered severe postnatal depression, and with the children, was admitted to a specialist mother and baby unit. There was a family portrait of Malcolm, Maria, Jack and the twins, April and Augusta, taken by a society photographer, shortly after Maria and the twins returned home. The couple sat on a Regency striped sofa, with eleven-year-old Jack standing behind them. Maria had a baby in each arm, and wore her push present – a string of perfect Tahitian pearls. Her glorious Titian curls were arranged over one shoulder but the eyes that looked out at

Malbister

the camera were dulled, and her expression, which should have been one of joy, was of wistful regret.

The twins had her colouring, but none of her charm. I suspected that Judith Goddard had shaped their personalities, sending them off to the right schools and making them all too aware of their father's wealth and status.

In 2009, early one morning in May, Maria left the Belsize park home before the family woke up. She was never seen again.

To give Goddard his due, he went to the police and made a huge fuss, offering a reward for Maria's safe return. This was before he was rich enough to make kidnapping viable. The police searched CCTV cameras, and tracked Maria through London and on to a commuter train. There was no sign of her getting off that train, at any of the stops, or when it returned. She simply vanished into thin air.

The Gambini family, one of the wealthiest in the Veneto region, were inconsolable. Maria's sister, Thalia, and her parents launched an appeal, but seven years later, she had never returned; never been in contact and Goddard began the paperwork to declare his wife legally dead. Before that process completed, Maria's father died of a heart attack and a year later her mother died of cancer. The twins visited their Italian grandparents once, as toddlers, and Judith, now both their nurse and grandmother, ensured contact was minimal with their mother's family.

Judith certainly knew how to make her presence felt. She was scowling at Matt and Freya, who were making a point of ignoring her. They had moved across to the window and their heads were together, as they looked down the escarpment towards the broch.

Matt turned to Goddard and asked, 'How long have those pines been there?'

Chapter 29

Goddard looked at my son and his mouth fell open. I didn't get the reference, and what did trees have to do with my sister going missing, anyway?

Freya spoke first. 'Most of the conifer forests planted in Caithness back in the 1980s were cut down a long time ago. They're not indigenous species and the companies that planted them as a tax break ignored the fact they were planting on peat – which is currently protected. I thought none of those trees still stood.' She shrugged, 'I was obviously mistaken.'

Matt continued, 'Given that Orkney, across the water, thrives on heritage tourism, there's a project to map the brochs in the north Highlands. The one over there, beside the trees is almost intact, and the chances are that the peat around it must house at least one ancient burial site. Peat preserves human remains for hundreds of years, and I'm surprised anyone would let a digger anywhere near it. In fact, the chance to see it, was why I came north to join Mum.'

Judith Goddard was scowling so hard, her brows knit together. Her son was listening intently, though, and I wondered what was running through his mind.

Malbister

I returned to the matter in hand. 'I came to Caithness because Kate phoned me, and I heard an argument between you. I don't know if she did so intentionally, or accidentally, but what I heard alarmed me. When I got here, she said you would be angry at me turning up and she begged me to leave, which I did. That doesn't stop me worrying about my sister, and I'm staying in the area until I know what's happened.'

I turned to the twins, 'Why did you have your stepmother's phone? And did you have it the day you slashed my bike tyres?'

One twin had taken a sandwich and a plate, and was busy deconstructing it, removing cucumber and picking the lettuce out. The other was looking nonchalant. I suspected she was the ringleader. 'So?' she said, 'I borrow her phone to order things. She keeps the shopping list on it. I needed some stuff. I was going to give it back. Besides, she's got the other one.'

Goddard said, 'What other one, Gussie?'

Augusta shot him a wary look. 'The one she keeps in her vanity case, in the wardrobe. The one we're not supposed to know about. It's a cheap one.'

'Where is it? Show us.'

We trooped after her. She climbed the open tread stairs to the upper level and pushed open the double doors into the master suite. There were separate dressing areas—Kate's was to the left. I wondered if it had been originally designed for Maria. She pushed open a sliding wardrobe door and pulled out Kate's battered vanity case. The case was a Christmas present from Mum, many years ago, and sat ill alongside the Vuitton luggage in the overhead storage area. She handed the case to Goddard, who set it down on the bed and tried to open it. It was locked. Katie had got wise to the twins. Augusta went to the dressing table, and returned with a hairpin, which she used to open the lock.

Inside the case were letters from Mum; her travelling make up case and a cheap phone, with its charger.

He took it and plugged the charger into the wall, and switched the phone on. The home screen asked for a password. 'Try her date of birth,' I suggested.

That didn't work. Mum's date of birth? 22/08/1950. That didn't work either. Malcolm looked at the phone as if it was going to bite him. The quiet twin, April, took the phone from him and tapped six digits in. It switched on.

'I watched her do it, 'she said.

The phone showed no outgoing or incoming calls – only a series of texts, which looked illegible. Kate was using some sort of code. They were all to one number, which none of the Goddard family recognised – but I did. Why on earth was Kate communicating in code, on a burner phone, with my husband?

Chapter 30

If I wasn't worried before, I was now. I took the phone and checked the list of texts to find the date they were sent. The last one was the same day as the call to my number. I was itching to ring Kevin, but I wasn't going to do so anywhere near Malcolm Goddard.

He was looking at me, but it was more like looking through me. I kept thinking he must have had something to do with her vanishing act, but the look on his face was more like worry than guilt. If anything, I'd guess he was scared.

'What have the police said?' Matt asked.

'They think she's run off with Ricci. He's been looking for a chance to cause trouble for years,' Judith Goddard snapped.

'What is he to you?' I asked.

'He's my brother-in-law,' Goddard said. 'Guiseppe Ricci is married to Thalia Gambini. Both of them accused me of doing away with Maria. Ricci's stirred up trouble since the day she went missing.'

'He went so far as to apply for custody of the girls,' Judith added. 'I put a stop to that pretty damn quick. They belong with us, not with their grandparents in Italy. Certainly not with their aunt and her damn husband. The man's a criminal anyway. He was in prison for fraud five years ago.'

Joe Ricci had given me a carefully edited version of the truth. Now I started to wonder if our first meeting was the coincidence it appeared to be?

'Joe Ricci also seems to have vanished,' I said. 'But your mother and your son ordered him out of town the night before he disappeared. Has anyone checked with the Norseman Hotel? When did he check out? He was supposed to be staying in the Pentland in Thurso last night, but Mrs Goddard cancelled the reservation.

I glowered at Judith Goddard, who looked at me calmly and said, 'You might not have noticed this, but there are officially two Mrs Goddards, and I certainly didn't ring the Pentland Hotel, much as I wanted to.'

The police had added two and two together and, in their opinion, it made four. Kate left Malbister, joined Ricci and they gave all of us the slip. No doubt they would turn up. Right at this moment I was no wiser than Malcolm Goddard. It bothered me that she had neither her own iPhone nor the cheap burner.

'Where's her handbag?' I asked.

Gussie opened another door. 'Which one?' she asked. The ten shelves were packed with designer bags, most of them costing several months' salary for most people. I scanned the shelves, looking for her Mulberry Bayswater. I found it jammed in a corner of the bottom shelf, and pulled it out. I upended it on the bench. Inside was her makeup pouch, her wallet and keys. I opened the wallet, which contained a hundred pounds in twenty-pound notes; a current account card and two credit cards.

'What's missing?' I asked.

Goddard shook his head. 'I don't understand. If she was

Malbister

leaving me, she'd have taken her car or her handbag, surely?'

'She didn't have her car, did she?' I said, turning to Jack Goddard. 'You have the keys to it, don't you? I saw you with it the night before she went missing. You took the twins into town.'

Goddard glared at his son. 'What the hell were you playing at? '

Gussie spoke up.' You were holding that dinner for the Shaikhs, and you sent us all upstairs. We got fed up and wanted something to do. I asked Jack to take us to the supermarket to get stuff. I knew where she keeps the car keys.'

The police version was that Ricci must have driven to the gates of Malbister and picked up Kate. They drove to Dunnet Head and switched vehicles, leaving the showy stolen Maserati behind. But where had they gone next?

We went outside, but instead of climbing into Morag, Matt and Freya headed down to the broch, despite a warning from Goddard that it wasn't safe. Matt had his research brain in gear, and ignoring Goddard he strode down the hill. A few moments after he reached the broch, he turned back, shouting 'Get the police out here now! There's a body in there!'

Chapter 31

Within an hour, a police officer was posted on the gates of Malbister and another was in charge of blue and white incident tape being placed across the entrance to the broch. They needed to wait for the Crime Scene Manager, SOCO team and the forensic experts to come up from Inverness, so we were herded back into Malbister House, where the local police took our names, addresses, dates of birth and our relationship to the deceased.

I confirmed I was Wendy Latimer, currently of no fixed abode, but about to take up a place at Sheffield Hallam University in September. My date of birth is 3rd June, 1972. I was working as a temp for Joe Ricci, who I met for the first time five days ago, by chance.

I was relieved the body in the broch wasn't my sister. The thought flashed through my head when Matt spoke. Surely, if Kate was dead, I would have known? Some sort of instinct? We might not have been the closest of sisters, but blood is thicker than water, and she knew she could always turn to me.

The police wouldn't tell me anything, but looking past the blue tape at the body lying in a pool of drying blood, I recognised Joe Ricci, who had been very much alive the night before last. The problem with that was that I was possibly the last person to see him alive, and in the eyes of the police, a suspect.

Malbister House was more than the Goddard home—it was also a business centre, and they ushered us into the office wing. I realised inside why he'd commissioned the new building. It was in the shape of a letter E, with two wings off the central atrium. The residential block was to the right and the business premises to the left. The central part included two guest suites. We were shown into a conference room with a vast table and a cathedral window. It was open plan and the table was surrounded by break out spaces. One of these had an L shape sofa and a coffee table. At the far end of the conference room was a water cooler and a coffee machine. Matt fetched us cups of ice-cold water, and I noticed the police were keeping us in small groups. Malcolm Goddard and his family were sent into the residential wing, and told to remain there until everyone was interviewed. I'd have been more comfortable had we been told to stay in Morag, but from the look of things, we were going to be here for a long time.

I looked out from one window which overlooked the stand of conifers and the broch, and crossed the room to look at the old Malbister Lodge. I'd done enough work with Kev to know a bit about buildings, and I wondered why there had been objections to restoring the old house. It must have looked impressive in its day—Annie Swanson said it was late 19th Century, so surely it didn't enjoy the same listed status as a Georgian building, or the ancient broch, for that matter. Part of the frontage still looked intact, and to the side were outbuildings: stables; a barn, a keeper's cottage and kennels. Katie had said there were gun dogs, and presumably someone was employed to care for them.

We watched as the Police Scotland vehicles arrived, one by one, including a plain black van, which I presumed would be used to transport the body to the mortuary in Inverness.

By five o clock, people in white cover all suits with covers over their shoes and hair, were all over the broch.

I got the feeling that the same officers who dismissed Kate's disappearance as a family tiff and nothing to worry about, were now taking this much more seriously. Where was she? Did Joe have something to do with it? And how on earth had he ended up here, of all places?

The DCI in charge was a woman, Linda Macleod. She wore a black linen suit, and a plain black top underneath the jacket, and her voice had a sing song quality, that indicated she came from the Western Isles. Her red hair was caught back in a clamp and tendrils escaped from it, blown by the air conditioning in the building. She wore a wedding ring and round her neck was a small gold pendant and chain.

Almost immediately she dismissed Matt and Freya. Their boarding passes and coach tickets showed they had not been in the county at the time Joe Ricci died. Matt flatly refused to leave, but Freya accepted the offer of a taxi to take her to Scrabster and the ferry to Stromness. She collected her rucksack from Morag and from the window, I watched Matt put his arms around her and kiss her goodbye. She left behind a note in a sealed envelope, to be handed to the SOCO team. 'Just a few observations about what Matt and I saw inside. And a comment about the trees nearby. Nothing to worry about, Wendy,' she said.

'She's a nice girl,' I said to Matt. 'Serious relationship? I thought you were dead against settling down too young?'

He grinned. 'When I said all of that, I hadn't met Freya. I'm going to stick around for a few days and then I've to get

Malbister

myself to Stromness to meet her family.'

'Does your dad know?'

'He picked us up from Heathrow and put us on the coach north,' he said. 'Mum, what's going on between the two of you?'

'I think you'd better ask him that,' I replied.

'I did,' he replied. 'Has Grandad been making trouble again? Dad said you hadn't checked out any new rental places and you've taken a post grad place up north. Why didn't you look for a post grad place in London? You could easily commute or study online.'

'Your dad had other ideas,' I replied. 'He was the one who took a live-in job, with no space for us to be together. I just decided to take Morag and have a break.'

'You will go back, won't you?' For the first time, he stopped being a capable young man, and I saw the boy he still was, underneath.

'I don't know. I was taking time out to think, then all of this happened.' I looked over to where Linda Macleod was standing and noticed she was beckoning me over.

The young detective constable with her introduced himself as Michael McLean. I thought about the cliché—you know you're getting old when the police look like schoolboys. He wore a charcoal grey suit, with a pale lilac shirt and plain grey silk tie. I wondered if his mother or his girlfriend picked it out.

He took his place at the table. There was some sort of digital recorder on the table between them and me. 'This interview is to gather your witness statement. Don't worry,' Linda Macleod said. I wondered if I'd looked alarmed?

'We need to check some details,' she began. 'When did you last see Joe Ricci?'

'We worked together on a presentation at the Norseman

Hotel on the evening of the 7th of June. He let me use his bathroom to get ready before the meeting, but I had my motorhome parked round the corner and I said goodnight to him at ten o clock.'

DC McLean wrote in his notebook. DCI McLeod looked thoughtful, and took a sip from the cup of water beside her.

'So, you wouldn't be surprised to find your finger marks in his hotel room?' she said.

I nodded.

'Why did you need to use the room to get ready?' McLean asked.

'Have you ever tried to wash your hair and shower in a motorhome bathroom?' I asked him.

'How long had you known Mr Ricci, Mrs Latimer?' Linda Macleod asked.

'I met him on my way north,' I replied. 'I set off on June 3rd. Nobody remembered it was my birthday, and I'd handed back the keys to my home.'

'Ah, yes,' she replied. '27, Denmark Crescent, Bath. Your previous address before you became homeless?'

I nodded.

'There is a note about your reporting Mr Ricci missing last night? Why did you do that?'

'I was supposed to be working with him at another meeting in the Pentland Hotel in Thurso, yesterday evening. I'd seen his Maserati in the car park of Dunnet Head lighthouse, but hadn't seen him in it, and I was concerned something might have happened to him. He wasn't at the Pentland when I showed up to set up. The hotel staff told me the meeting room and his accommodation had been cancelled by a Mrs Goddard.'

'When did you first meet Mr Ricci?' McLean asked.

'I met him in the Cheltenham Motorway Services on the

fourth of June, just five days ago. He came across to look at my motorhome. He said he used to work for the company that designed it. We just talked about the van, really.' As I spoke, I realised how lame a story it must sound. It was the truth, but it didn't sound particularly convincing.

'Did he offer you work at that point?' MacLeod's eyebrows were raised. She sipped her water again, and glanced at the Apple watch on her left wrist.

'Not at that point,' I replied.

'Presumably you met him again?' There was an acerbic tone to her voice, now, and I sensed her patience was about to run out.

'Yes, I took a detour to Gretna on my way north, and he was parked there. We had a snack together. It was just a coincidence.'

'You didn't think there was anything suspicious about that? Might he have been following you?' I wondered what she was getting at.

She brushed an imaginary speck of dust from her jacket and picked up the pen beside her and squinted at it.

'Why did you drive north, Mrs Latimer?'

'I had a strange phone call from my sister.' I pulled the phone from my pocket and found the voicemail message. I pressed play. Wendy's voice and those sounds.

They listened intently. MacLeod frowned.

'I thought she was in some danger and I thought I'd better come and see how she was?'

'Is this something you would normally do? Doesn't it seem rash to drive the length of the country on a hunch? Wouldn't you need to take leave from your work?'

I shook my head. 'I was made redundant. My job finished last week. I was living in Morag, my motorhome, and I was going to spend the next two months doing temp work. I'd not seen my sister for ages, and I thought I might as well come and visit.'

McLeod made a steeple of her hands and rested her chin on her fingertips. 'What sort of reception did you get when you arrived?'

'Kate was scared of something. She told me it wasn't a good time and to leave before her husband came back. He was collecting guests from Wick Airport,' I said. 'I told her that I would be sticking around this area for a few days, until we had a chance to talk.'

'And did you? Talk, I mean?'

'No,' I replied.

'But you met Ricci again?'

'I thought I'd best be a tourist while I was here. I parked my van and took my bike to Whaligoe steps. I climbed down and ran into Kate's stepdaughters at the bottom. They ran past me up the steps and when I went back up, my bike tyres were slashed and they'd gone. I went into the café to ask if there was a bike shop where I could get them mended, and Jo Ricci was there. He gave me a lift back to Morag, my motorhome, and offered me a temp job for three evenings, handing out sales brochures and doing PR stuff.'

I sipped at my own cup of water. It was no longer cold, and it tasted brackish.

'You accepted an offer of work from a man you hardly knew?' MacLeod sounded sceptical. Beside her, McLean was scribbling in his notebook.

'Temp work is just that,' I replied, 'temporary. I need the money. Three evenings of four hour meetings at ten pounds an hour. A hundred and twenty pounds for twelve hours work is neither here nor there—it simply pays for my fuel.'

McLean got up and went across to the coffee machine, returning with a cup and saucer and a biscuit. 'Sorry, I missed lunch and my blood sugar's a bit low,' he murmured. 'Anyone want something?'

MacLeod glanced at her watch. 'Let's get this over with first,' she said.

McLean bit into his biscuit and got crumbs on his tie. He blushed. 'We have a statement from the manager of the Norseman. He said your meeting ended badly—that Mrs Judith Goddard and Mr Jack Goddard not only broke it up, but also tried to cancel the rest of the meetings. Was that your impression?'

'Yes,' I said. 'They intimidated the people who came to the sales pitch. They said that if anyone bought the holiday lodges, or tried to put them on land that they leased, that they would be in trouble. They nearly all handed the sales brochures back.'

'How did Joe Ricci react to that?'

'He was angry,' I said. 'But to be honest, I was upset, because the Goddards have been bullying my sister, and they were trying to intimidate me too.'

'What did you do at the end of the evening?' MacLeod's eyes were boring into me. They were a pale green, and I got the feeling that she didn't believe me.

'We had a drink in the bar, and then I picked up my bag from the meeting room and went back to my motor home. I went to bed and the last thing I remember was checking my phone just before midnight, and setting my alarm. I needed to start moving early.'

They looked at one another.

'The CCTV from the hotel shows Joe Ricci leaving the hotel around half past eleven, and driving away in his car. He didn't return to the hotel. Where do you think he would have gone?'

I shrugged. 'I know he was angry at what happened, but

as far as I knew, he went up to his room and went to bed. I saw the car at Dunnet Head the next day, but I didn't see him. That's why I told the officers last night.'

'They went to the hotel to check that out, before the body was found,' McLean said. 'The day manager told them that Mr Ricci didn't check out. His bill was pre-paid, so the manager got the maid to pack his bag and they left it behind reception.'

'We need to know what Joe Ricci did between the time he left the hotel and the moment of his death. For the record, are you sure you didn't see him after you said goodnight?'

Chapter 32

I knew I told the truth, but I wasn't sure they believed me. Matt came across and reminded them that we hadn't eaten. It was past seven in the evening, and the police had yet to interview the Goddard family.

The prospect of hanging round Malbister as a prime suspect terrified me, and I felt sick, but Matt didn't need to suffer on my behalf. The detectives had the registration details of Morag, and I gave my word not to leave the county and to check in with the police station in Wick the next morning. We headed back to Thurso, to our pitch. It meant that Matt could get his washing done, and we picked up a takeaway to eat in the van. Matt nipped into a corner shop to get some beer. I packed up my bed, so we had the table to sit across and I watched my son fork up his food and eat with obvious relish. I picked at my pakora and rice, unable to taste a thing.

'Mum, who was the man in the broch?' Matt asked, between mouthfuls. 'And how come you got to know him?'

I sighed. I'd already been grilled by the two police detectives, and now my own son was interrogating me. 'He called himself Joe Ricci, and he chatted me up about Morag.

He kept calling her Vanozza, and he said he designed her and got the bathroom wrong.'

Matt chuckled. 'I won't disagree with him about the bathroom. Have you looked in the manual?'

I'd forgotten about the manual. Matt fished it out of the glove compartment: right enough the title page said Goldstar Vanozza 3.0 litre.

Matt was busy with his phone. He found the Wikipedia page. It included a picture of the design team, which included a much younger Joe, along with several other people. His name, however, was given as Joe Richards. Wasn't it a Mr Richards who reported the Maserati stolen?

A quick search of Companies House listed Joe Richards and his brother George Richards as former directors of Goldstar Motorhomes, with the former resigning in 2007 and the latter remaining on the board until 2015.

'Okay, what else do you know?' Matt took a swig of his beer and leaned his elbows on the table.

'Only what Malcolm Goddard told us. He was Goddard's brother-in-law through marriage, and I got the feeling there was bad blood between them.' I nibbled a poppadum and sipped at my beer.

'So, what do you know about Goddard's wife, before Aunt Kate?' he asked.

'Maria Gambini? Again, what they told us. She sounded pretty vulnerable.'

He was busy with the internet again. He shoved the phone across to me. The headline from 2010 read:

MISSING HEIRESS LEAVES FAMILY IN PIECES

Enzo Gambini yesterday renewed his appeal for his missing daughter, Maria Gambini Goddard to contact her family.

Maria Gambini left the family home in London in 2009 and nobody has seen her since she boarded a commuter train and disappeared. Her absence left her twin daughters without a mother, and her husband, financier Malcolm Goddard of Falconbury Investments offered a reward for information leading to her return to her family.

Maria Gambini, together with her father and her sister Thalia Gambini Ricci, own a controlling share in Azienda Leopardate, the luxury goods company founded by her grandparents in 1952. Her husband sought to get control of his wife's shares in the firm, but encountered obstacles in the Italian courts.

When reporter Carla da Mosta suggested that Gambini was suffering from post-natal depression, her father said that he blamed her husband and his family for making his daughter's life a misery. Shortly before her disappearance, she told her father she intended to take the twins and return to the family home near Venice. He is convinced that she is in danger and has met with the Italian and British police to escalate the search for the missing mother of two.

'So, Mum, what do you make of that? Does that sound like someone who would go and top herself? She had a family to go home to, and she wasn't some poor helpless wife without any source of income.'

I had the uncomfortable feeling that there was a subtext to what Matt was saying. Mum defied Dad to take her little part time job, so she had a bit of money of her own. She hated having to go to him to buy a pair of shoes or to help us out, but she never made the sort of money that would allow her to leave him. I had a decent job, but it was well below what I was capable of doing. Maria Gambini was rich and had a career—so what really happened to her?

'Matt, the police didn't tell me how he died. You saw inside the broch—what do you think he died of? I saw blood, but I couldn't tell beyond that. Was he stabbed?'

He took some time to answer. 'Mum, while they were speaking to you, they took your keys and had the forensics team going over Morag. They were looking for something, but I don't think they found it.'

'What? Why didn't you tell me before?' I asked. I'd noticed Morag was a bit untidy, but the thought of the police going through my stuff made me feel sick.

'Joe Ricci was shot. They were looking for a gun.'

'Gun? Do you honestly think I'd have a gun?'

He laughed. 'The only time I've ever seen you fire anything was at a funfair, and you missed every single shot. Chill. '

Motive, means, opportunity. I had no apparent motive. I had no gun, and I hadn't seen Joe after ten o clock two nights ago.

On the other hand, Joe died on Malcolm Goddard's land, and there were plenty of guns in the locked cabinet in the hallway. The guests had security – and Jack was sent to look for Katie in case she walked in the way of the clay pigeon guns. Malcolm Goddard had his second wife declared dead and wanted control of her part of a big company. That sounded like motive, means and opportunity to me.

I wondered how the day was ending across the county in Malbister.

Chapter 33

June 10th, 2019

I spent another restless night. Matt offered to take the over-cab bunk, but I reckoned he'd long since outgrown it and he cleared the table, did the dishes and turned the dining area back into the double bed. I took myself across to the shower block to rescue his washing, which was now dry, and shower and changed into pyjamas before bedtime. I didn't want to scare Matt by sleeping in my vest and knickers.

I scrambled into the over cab bunk just before eleven. It was still daylight outside, and we were a mere eleven days from the solstice. I wondered what Caithness was like in midwinter when the days were short?

My son snored happily, sprawled diagonally across the double bed. I envied his ability to switch off and unwind, but then I remembered, guiltily, that he had travelled the length of Britain over the past twenty-four hours, and arrived to find his mum embroiled in a murder inquiry. If anything would make you desperate for a good sleep, it would be that.

In contrast, I lay on my back, wondering where my sister was and fearing the worst. I must have drifted off around two a.m. as the sun briefly dipped then rose again. Matt woke me with the whistling kettle, around half past seven.

My plan was to check in with the police station and to take a trip with Matt before he caught the ferry to join Freya, later that evening. We packed up and were on the road before 9am, reaching Wick Police Station half an hour later.

McLean and MacLeod had driven back to Inverness late last night and were not planning to return until this afternoon. I wrote down my plans for the day and promised to return if called. Then we set off for the Camster Cairns.

We drove for about seven miles and I worried about taking Morag on a single-track road with awkwardly small passing places. Matt was enthusiastic. 'These cairns are over five thousand years old. They're older than the pyramids. Neolithic masterpieces.'

'So why haven't I heard of them?'

He laughed. 'You have, only you don't know it. Remember when you used to read me bits from 'Lord of the Rings?' The Barrow Downs were based on them. Tolkien was a mad keen angler and he used to fish at Helmsdale and in Caithness. Ever wondered about the place names? Helmsdale could be Helm's Deep. The map of Middle Earth looks like the map of the North Highlands seen in a mirror.

He was less keen about the massive wind farm on the other side of the road. 'What the hell's going on here? Can you imagine that being allowed at Stonehenge or in Pompeii?'

We found a parking spot and got out to explore the cairns. The great whale shaped structures were flanked by boardwalks. Matt was beside himself, reminding me of the child he'd been.

Ten years ago, when he was a teenager, we took the family in Morag to Stonehenge. It was a day out for us: a rare

Malbister

treat for all four of us to be together without Kevin having to tear himself away for some work-related crisis. He was between jobs and we had a fortnight off to do a staycation, using the motorhome to travel to places we'd always intended to see, but never had time to visit. I wondered if Stonehenge was the start of my son's passion for the past?

He called me over. 'I can't believe that these aren't on the UNESCO World Heritage radar. Freya reckons, with Orkney being big on heritage tourism, that these should be at the top of the list. There's a Broch restoration project group around here. We were hoping to meet up with them.'

I had my heart in my mouth when he strapped a head torch on and scrambled inside the cairn. I should be used to seeing him taking risks – from labouring for Kevin, climbing ladders with loads of bricks, to heading off to places all over the world. I've always been proud of my kids, and the fact they have two parents who love them unconditionally, would back them in anything they choose to do, and don't have unreasonable expectations. When Amy once asked me what I hoped they would be when they grew up, I said, firmly, 'Happy and healthy. Do what works for you, and your dad and I will always be proud of you.'

Different from Katie and me. Mum loved us both unconditionally, but Dad made it all too clear he expected us to do better in life than he had, and he never forgave me for marrying Kevin. When Katie landed Malcolm Goddard, he preened himself over his daughter's good fortune, to the point of hurting Mum by insisting she interrupted her chemotherapy to go to the wedding. If Goddard was prepared to go to the cost of a private flight, the least she could do was be there for the big day.

I took an afternoon off and booked the personal shopper in the store to help Mum choose her mother of the bride outfit. The treatment had ruined her once lustrous blonde hair, and she had lost two stones, and looked like a puff of wind would blow her away. We made an occasion of the afternoon, with sparkly juice—she declined alcohol—and canapes. Katie wanted to join us, but at the last minute, had to call off. I watched as Mum's cheerful mood collapsed. The least my sister could have done was have one afternoon with her dying mother and her sister.

By four o clock, we'd found a flattering cloche hat, and a shot silk dress and jacket in a matching shade, and Ruth, the personal shopper, took a pair of silk court shoes to have dyed to match. I held Mum's hand – once so strong, and now pitifully fragile, like a broken bird in a velvet glove. 'Are you sure about this, Mum? What did the oncologist say about you going?'

'She wanted me to ask Katie to postpone the wedding until this round was over. I would...but your father would never forgive me.'

We were both in tears by then. Her one shot at a bit of extra time was taken from her by my father and my brother-in-law. She died soon after the wedding, and I hadn't forgiven either of them. Kevin had to put up with my impotent rage, but if he hadn't been there to talk sense into me, I might have done something I would later regret.

Mum moved into the hospice after Katie's wedding. She was devastated, and didn't want to see Dad. She said she blamed him for everything-not just Katie marrying a man who Mum reckoned would make her younger daughter's life miserable, but for all the petty things he had done over their forty-eight years of marriage.

'I watched him, Wendy. I watched him gloating about her so-called good fortune, and I realised I hated him. I don't have much time left, and I'm not spending any of it in that

Malbister

house, being preached to by him. I'm just glad you have Kevin. You're going to need him soon.'

Kevin and Dorothy got me through Mum's funeral. Dad appalled me by saying he couldn't cope and Mum wouldn't have wanted any fuss. He even suggested having no funeral service and just a quiet cremation at the end of the day. Malcolm and Katie were still overseas. She hadn't made it back for the end. I'd sat with Mum the night before she died, and left the hospice to catch some sleep, only to be rung at five am.

I'd picked up the phone from the bedside table, squinting at the screen, and pressed the answer symbol. 'Is that Wendy?'

'Yes,' I murmured.

'I'm sorry, Wendy, but your mum passed away a few minutes ago. I was checking in every few minutes and when I went in, she was gone. She passed in her sleep, if that's any comfort. I'm so sorry for your loss.'

Kevin stirred beside me and pulled me into his arms and held me while I cried. They'd always been good together, and I knew he felt Mum's loss as much as I did. He rang Matt at university and I told Amy, who took the day off school to be with me.

Mum's funeral let Dad see exactly how many people loved and valued my mother. The crematorium moved the service from the small chapel to the bigger one, when all of her colleagues from work turned up, along with her friends from evening classes and her keep fit class, and Kevin's side of the family.

She was cremated in the outfit she wore to Katie's wedding. There was poetry, and music. Matt did the reading and Kevin delivered the eulogy. Dad sat there in the front row, right at the end of the pew, and Matt positioned himself between us, tactfully.

Matt emerged from the chambered cairn, brushing dirt from his hair and clothes, but clearly delighted with what he'd seen. 'Wow,' he said. 'That place is amazing.' He looked at me. 'Why are you crying, Mum?'

I put my hand up to my face and realised it was wet with tears. 'I was thinking of your Nan. She was so proud of you,' I said.

He gave me a fierce hug. 'Come on, then. I've got plans for us.'

Chapter 34

There's a line from a poem that describes the tropical sea as pouring 'Bean green over blue.' Kevin and I had never been to the Caribbean – or anywhere exotic, come to think of that. I'd never seen a sea that matched that description until I drove over the causeway at Tongue and headed through the Geopark. This was Matt's day, and his treat. The sky overhead was the bluest I'd ever seen, with barely a cloud, and the sea could have been the Caribbean or the Aegean. The landscape was rugged and rocky, with a backdrop of mountains and mist. We drove past tiny settlements, including a pottery in the shape of a gypsy caravan on the very edge of the water. I saw Highland cattle grazing contentedly in the fields, and we were stuck for half an hour while a shepherd took a flock of sheep from a pasture on one side of the road, to hill pasture on the other side.

There was no sense of being in a hurry. I got irritated by other motorhome drivers and by the performance car drivers who raced past, without taking time to appreciate what was all around them. An open top Aston, racing in the opposite direction, almost put us in the ditch. I swore, tugging on the steering wheel to keep us on the road. It took another five miles for my heart to stop thumping, but how could anyone be so oblivious to all this?

We stopped to eat our sandwich lunch, and for the first time since I left home, I felt I was on a real holiday. I clinked coffee cups with Matt and said, 'Thanks – this is amazing.'

He smiled, and looked so like his dad at that moment, I felt a lump in my throat. 'I thought it was about time you saw some real rocks.'

'Matt – what exactly is a geopark?'

'It's all about community looking after this land,' he said. The area has unique features, but it's also home to the people who farm, and fish here, and run the small businesses. They're not here like holidaymakers are – short term. Their lives are all about this place, looking after it, caring for it and keeping it safe from idiots like Malcolm Goddard.'

I thought about Dunrobin – and about Malbister – where the owners didn't have a sense of community and threw people off their land.

'UNESCO supports projects like this, globally,' he explained, when we parked at Durness and walked down the steep path towards the sea. 'I want to show you this place,' he said, as we got to the entrance of Smoo Cave. I'd never seen an indoor waterfall before, and it took my breath away. 'It was formed by water getting through limestone and forming a weak sort of acid that bored into the rocks. Would you believe that rivers sometimes go into sink holes?' A boat, tied up, took people across and into the heart of the waterfall. I felt I was in a fantasy film. No CGI could capture what was in that cave.

We emerged afterwards and walked on the beach, marvelling at the beauty of the place, before returning to Morag and taking her to Balnakeil Craft Village. Annie Swanson had told me that Cocoa Mountain had the best hot

Malbister

chocolate in the world, and as we collected our cups, with foamed milk and cream and milk and white chocolate dripping down the sides, I knew she was right.

I was halfway through my heavenly drink when I saw the Range Rover pull up and Judith Goddard and the twins climb out.

Matt swore. 'Oh, for heavens' sake!' he said — or words to that effect. 'Do you think they've been following us?'

'I wouldn't put it past them,' I replied. 'They think I know where Katie is, and they seem to be on my tail, ruining things. I'm not letting them spoil this,' I said, inwardly realising they already had.

They were coming into the café, the twins darting to a free table in the opposite corner from us. Their grandmother was giving a complicated order at the counter, but all the while scowling across at us. She made no attempt to speak to me, thankfully. I sipped the last of my chocolate.

Matt said, 'I can text Freya to say I'm staying here for the time being, if you like? Or you can get Morag on the ferry and come to Orkney?'

It was tempting, but I hesitated. 'I need to know what's happened to your aunt. Tell you what, I'll come across as a foot passenger in a few days if you are hanging about?' What time is your ferry?'

He checked the timetable on his phone. 'It leaves at seven pm. I need to be there for half six. Sorry about the rush.'

We left the café, and I walked across to the Goddards. 'Is there any word of my sister?' I asked.

Judith Goddard scowled at me. 'I don't know and I care less,' she snapped.

I didn't pursue it, and we drove back to Thurso, the holiday mood spoiled. The blue sky vanished behind clouds and it was raining heavily as I parked at Scrabster and walked with Matt to the ticket office. He gave me a big hug, and hoisting his rucksack on his strong shoulders, he gave me a wave and was gone.

I walked back towards Morag, already feeling lonely. Matt had been a breath of fresh air, taking my mind off my worries and making me feel there was an ally against the world. I didn't have the money for another night on the campsite—just as well, as it was suddenly very busy. Instead, I parked beside the old fish shed on the waterfront, grabbed a waterproof and headed for the beach.

The man with the two black dogs was there again – possibly his evening ritual. The same runner came by, and they exchanged the same summons to the Comm, whatever it was. I was tempted to go for a drink, but remembered I was a lone female and it might not be wise. Instead, I walked on the sand, and looked out to sea, where the ferry was making its way to Orkney. I waved, knowing there was no way my son would see me. I fought back the sudden lump that came into my throat. 'Katie – where the hell are you?'

Chapter 35

When we were children, I wasn't bullied, but Katie was.

Mum used to wonder why, as a five-year-old, I was invited to the boys' parties, but seldom to the girls'? Other little girls would skip off in their party frocks, to events with pink cake, and girly party games and party bags containing sugar and spice and all things nice. In contrast, I wore dungarees and played at Star Wars and little boy games, returning home muddy with feathers in my hair. I was Princess Leia to Kevin's Han Solo, or the squaw tied to the tree that supposedly needed to be rescued.

At primary school, I was an odd one out among the girls. I had friends, but none of them were as close as Kevin and I were. At secondary school, the girls resented me at first, because at lunchtime, I played football with the boys, and hung out with them in the playground. Later, they realised I was their best hope of getting close enough to the lads to chat them up. I introduced at least two of Kevin's friends to their future wives. Kevin, however, refused to take the bait and always walked me home.

We were walking back from school one day when we saw Katie, still in primary, in a state of distress. I asked why she was crying, but she kept her chin down and refused to meet my eyes. Her school trousers were ripped at the knee and there were deep scratches on her nose and upper lip.

'Katie, have you been fighting?' I asked.

She shook her head, tears running down her face. Finally, she whispered, 'Don't tell Dad.'

'Okay if I tell Mum?'

She put both hands over her face and sobbed. Kevin, meanwhile, had looked around and spotted two girls looking daggers at my little sister. Before I could tell him not to, he strode over to them and demanded, 'was it you two who made her cry?'

They looked defiant in much the same way I noticed the Goddard twins looking at us today. He didn't let it drop. 'Why?' he demanded. They muttered something, keeping their eyes on the ground and slunk off.

She was simply too sweet and too pretty – and she'd beaten the others in an art competition they thought they should have won. They taunted her for being a 'Teacher's pet' all the way down the road. Once out of sight of the school, the taunts turned to blows, and she ran so fast to escape them, that she tripped over and hurt her face on the pavement.

We took her home and, as Mum was at work, I got out the TCP and cotton wool and cleaned her up, but the cut on her upper lip needed a stitch, so Kevin ran home to tell his mum, and she drove all of us to the minor injury unit at the hospital where she worked and got Katie seen by a doctor. Then she rang my Dad.

He was beside himself with rage. If anything happened to me, it was usually my fault. If his little princess got hurt, he took it out on everyone around him, and Mum came in for a row about going to work and not collecting us at the

Malbister

school gates.

Mum gently reminded him that Kevin would never allow any harm to come to Katie and me—and besides I was pretty good at handling myself anyway. Had Katie not stayed behind to collect her art prize, she would have been walking home with us – and not picked on by the jealous girls.

Dad went up to school and made the almightiest fuss, demanding to speak to the Art teacher and the Head, and accusing the two girls of assault. He even threatened legal action against the parents.

It all backfired on Katie, who was so miserable she looked for any excuse not to attend school. On the day we caught her playing truant, trying to hide in the park, we decided enough was enough. I got a book on assertiveness training from my form tutor, and after school each day, when we collected Katie, we did an exercise to build her confidence and Kevin's friend Arthur, who did judo, taught her some self-defence.

By the time she was in secondary school, she was less of a target, but there was a vulnerability about her that I didn't share, that never quite went away.

I wondered if that was why she was drawn to boys who treated her badly? Several times, when she was hurt, I had to stop Kevin from going after whoever had made her miserable.

Malcolm Goddard was just the latest in a long line of creeps.

I returned to my motorhome, to find a dark blue car with a police light parked alongside. 'Oh great,' I thought. 'No overnight parking – again.' Then MacLean and MacLeod got out.

'Mrs Latimer, might we have a word?'

Chapter 36

MacLean had been eating – there were pastry crumbs on his tie, and his smart suit was creased from sitting in the car. MacLeod was as elegant as before, this time in a sleeveless dress and flat pumps, and her expensive raincoat was folded neatly on the parcel shelf of the car.

They indicated Morag and I unlocked the van and ushered them in. Thankfully, Matt had folded the bed away, so they took seats at the table and I put the kettle on. They made no excuses about being on duty, and I knew they must have had a long and frustrating day.

MacLeod accepted a cup of decaffeinated tea, and I handed a mug of instant coffee to MacLean who took it in both hands. I offered my biscuit tin, and while MacLeod declined, MacLean took two custard creams. Growing lad, I thought.

'Joe Ricci was shot by a sniper's rifle,' MacLeod said. 'Your brother-in-law says it was an accident. His guests were Saudis, pretty high-profile people and close to their government. They had their own security detail with them, who were patrolling the grounds. It seems that Joe Ricci triggered the alarms and must have been hit by a stray bullet.

Malbister

The visitors have diplomatic immunity and the gunman left the country before anyone knew that they'd shot and killed an intruder.'

'Basically, we've been called off that case and the security services will be dealing with it from now on. It's above our pay grade. The Home Office have put a news blackout on it for the moment.'

'However, we still don't know when he reached Malbister and why he went there in the night, in the first place.'

McLean swallowed a mouthful of custard cream and said, 'Have you had any word from your sister?'

'I've had no call or message from her since I last saw you. I'm worried about her.' That was the understatement of the century. If Goddard's guests were capable of shooting down an intruder, what was to stop them killing my sister?

'I'm being followed by her mother-in-law. I took my son to Durness today, and she arrived shortly after we did, along with the twins.'

They nodded, and McLean took his notebook and pen out.

I told them about the twins taking Katie's phone but I didn't mention the burner phone with the coded texts. Instinct told me not to involve Kevin in this, at least until I had to.

'Where do you think she might be, Mrs Latimer? Mr Goddard doesn't seem to know who her friends are.'

'That's because he's got between her and her family,' I snapped. 'When they moved to Malbister, we hardly heard from her, apart from Christmas cards. And she no longer has any friends. He's made sure of that!'

Those Christmas cards were slick printed family group pictures, with Malcolm and Katie seated, with the twins kneeling at their feet and Jack and Judith standing behind them. The signatures were pre-printed. The cards should have looked personal, but they had the opposite effect. It was as if the Goddard brand had stolen my sister and put her in their corporate picture, leaving a gap behind in our family. It was a parody of the photograph that featured Maria Gambini.

'Are there any other relatives who might help her?' MacLeod asked. 'Your husband? Your father?'

MacLean carefully placed the burner phone in a clear plastic evidence bag on the table. 'There's only one phone number on this. Goddard says that he showed it to you. The text messages appear to be in some sort of code.'

Damn. I'd meant to ring Kevin – but when I'd tried earlier in the day, the number was engaged and I sent a text asking him to call me. I fished out my phone and checked. There were three missed calls from him. Mobile coverage on the road we were on today was uneven.

'Can I have a few minutes?' I didn't wait for their response, but nipped out of Morag and walked to the sea wall, hitting call and hoping he picked up.

He answered on the third ring. 'Wendy, love, are you okay?'

'I've got the police with me. Katie's gone missing and they've got a burner phone with your number on it and text messages in some sort of code. What's going on?' I darted a look back towards Morag, but they were deep in conversation.

'It's an old phone of hers – one from years ago. She put a pay as you go Sim in it, and we agreed if she needed to contact you or me, and couldn't use her own phone for some reason, that she would keep it safe and we worked out a code. Remember that lesson we had about Beale cyphers at

Malbister

school?'

'Vaguely. Why didn't you tell me? She's my sister, after all.'

'I was going to. The codes translate to 'I don't feel safe, or I need Wendy to call me or I'm in real danger.' It was a get me out of here panic button. Do you want me to speak to the police?'

'In a minute. I'm still trying to get my head round all of this. How long ago did you set this up?'

'The last time she visited your dad, just before he sold the house and moved to Spain. She said she was scared of Goddard's family. The twins had a habit of pinching her phone and reading her messages. She wanted to know how to secure the phone so they were blocked out. Amy gave her a lesson in mobile security. Kate told me that she was just glad her cats were with Betsy, so the twins couldn't do something nasty to them.'

'And she didn't tell me?' I wailed.

'She didn't tell you because she knows you too well. You'd have dropped everything to ride to the rescue—just like you've done—and she was scared something bad would happen to you.'

The penny dropped. After that strange call, I'd done exactly that. I'd surprised myself, doing things I wouldn't have dared only a few weeks ago.'

'When did she send the last message and what was it?' I was scared now, and my knees were shaking.

'It was 'I'm in real danger,' and she sent it on the 3rd. I tried to call you, and I rang Police Scotland.'

'Okay, Kevin, I'm going to hand you over to the police officers.'

I returned to Morag, switched the phone onto speaker and set it on the table.

MacLeod said, 'Kevin Latimer?'

'I'm here,' he said. 'What happened to my call to Police Scotland on the 3rd of this month? My sister-in-law sent a message to say she was in some sort of danger. I rang your hotline and someone was going to check on her.'

MacLeod told MacLean to check, and he sat in Morag's passenger seat to radio it in. He returned and said: 'Two officers were sent to check the house, but she told them it was a false alarm. Goddard was there.'

'She wouldn't have said anything about feeling scared, in front of him,' I said.

Macleod asked Kevin, 'Other than the coded message, did she ring you at all? You wouldn't know if she was in contact with someone called Joe Ricci?'

'You mean my boss?' Kevin asked.

'Your boss? I thought you were working with Mrs Couper?' Something wasn't making any sense.

'I'm working for JTC Holdings,' he said. 'Mrs Couper's on the board, but my project manager is Ricci. I've been working on his tiny house prototype since the day you were told you were likely to be made redundant. I was at the interview, that evening. I've been staying on site, down here in Devon since the work started. I thought you knew. I came up to see Matt when he got back from Jordan. I told him to tell you. Or is he just so loved up with that Orcadian girl that it slipped his mind?'

MacLeod and MacLean exchanged a look. 'Okay, Mr Latimer. You've been a great help. We will need to speak to you again – can we just check your number? And, did you tell Ricci that your sister-in-law was Mrs Goddard? Or that your wife was going to visit her?'

'Not that I can remember. I did say something about my wife living in the motorhome and he said if the prototype

Malbister

that I'm working on was successful, that we could buy it at a discount.'

Before they left, MacLeod said, 'Your husband was very helpful, Mrs Latimer. He's given us the missing link. We'll be in touch.'

Katie was still missing. Kevin wasn't with Mrs Couper. I didn't know what on earth was going on.

Chapter 37

I thought back to that night – the day when my world fell to bits. I was completely rattled by those three grey men, who pronounced the end of my career in retail management without turning a hair. My rented house—which I'd worked hard to make a home—was about to be snatched from me by a greedy estate agent. It turned out later that the mystery buyer was none other than Shelby and her fiancé. When Kevin arrived home late, from working for a woman I knew had a penchant for fit, younger men, it was the last straw.

I rang him again after the police left. I was irritated by how the sound of his voice made me feel. I stopped being capable of standing up to the world, and I felt insecure about how far away he was, out of reach in an emergency.

I asked him about the job. I should have done so at the time, but I was furious at him, and when he'd said, 'I've got the chance of some work on a project. Only thing is, it's away from here, and they want me to start before the lease runs out here, and you finish work. The company are going to put me up in a B&B, but I think it's going to be pretty basic. You might want to go and visit your dad? Give you a chance to put things right with him? You could see Amy on the way

Malbister

back?'

Thinking back, those weren't actually bad suggestions. I'd been angry with Dad for moving away, and I'd said things I regretted. I badly needed a proper holiday, and the sensible thing would have been to negotiate a bit more time in the house to find another rental. I worried about Amy, away from home in a strange country. Instead, when Dad made an excuse not to let me visit, I let his nastiness about Kevin get under my skin.

Now, I was listening.

'I was doing the outhouse conversion for that Mrs Couper,' he began. That cheered me up—if she was that Mrs Couper and he wasn't calling her by her first name, it changed a lot.

'Anyway, she liked the new home gym and the hot tub area, and she said that JTC Holdings had been approached by a start-up. They had plans for flat pack prefab holiday lodges, from a guy who specialised in fitting out motorhomes and yachts, but they hadn't yet got anyone to build them.

'The guy – Joe Ricci – was there that evening, and he let me have a look at the plans. It turned out he was from the company that built our Morag, and we discussed what it was like to live in a motorhome for months. I said that if they were putting the prototype out to tender, that I'd like to get the chance to build it. I reckoned I could get the lads involved, and it could give us a few months of work, with the option to get the contract for the build, longer term.

'He was a bit cagey, said that there was likely to be a patent involved, and that meant rather than go to tender, he wanted the prototype built in house, and he'd been invited along that evening to take a look at my work. I thought nothing of it, but the next day, when I went into work, Mrs Couper said the job was mine, if I wanted it. The only problem was that, as their target sales area would initially be Devon and Cornwall, that they'd leased a unit in an industrial estate down there, and they'd need the workers to stay close by. There was a B&B close by that they'd rented for the summer. I went down and had a look, and reckoned that you'd hate it, and it might be better to bring Morag down, if you were joining me for the summer. But the next thing, you said you wanted time to think, and I worried your dad had said something again. I thought the best thing was to say nothing and wait until you'd calmed down. The next thing I knew, you'd signed up for that course and said we needed to take a break.

'Anyway, I came down here and the job started. Ricci came down to give me a hand, and the lads arrived once the job they were subcontracted on finished. They're great little holiday homes.'

'I know,' I said. 'I was helping to try and sell some of them in the Highlands. At least, I was supposed to be – before Ricci got himself killed.'

Silence. I pictured Kevin's jaw hitting the floor.

'Kevin, how much did you tell Joe Ricci about me and my sister?'

There was an indignant muttering on the other end of the line. I was starting to wish this was a video call. I can always tell when Kevin is being less than truthful, and it generally involves money. I might miss him, but it didn't mean I'd forgiven him.

'I didn't have to tell him anything. He already knew about Kate. His wife, Thalia, came down to look at the prototype, and they took us all out for a meal. She told me her sister was the second wife of Malcolm Goddard – the one that went missing and was declared dead, before he got together with Kate. She said that she'd expected Maria to take the twins

Malbister

and leave him, and she'd even organised a car to come and collect them, but the next thing she heard was that Maria walked out and vanished into thin air. Then she asked me how I'd feel if the same thing happened to Kate?'

'And what did you tell her?' I asked, already knowing the answer.

'I said that Kate was scared of something and I mentioned the burner phone to her. Then that message came in. I was in the middle of the build, so all I could do was alert the police, but Ricci promised he would head north and see what was going on for himself. '

'So, you sent him? How did he know to look for me?' My stomach was in knots.

'Do you remember that time Amy took our phones to set up the apps? She put a tracker on both of us, as a joke. He borrowed his brother's flashy car and said he was going to follow you up north. He said he wasn't able to get into Goddard's place – but you might manage it. I'm sorry, Wendy. I really am.'

It was making sense now—all of those chance meetings on the road north were actually planned. How on earth had I not twigged before now?

'Why didn't you mention this to the police?' I said.

'It doesn't look good, love. If we've got any sense, we need to step back from the Goddards. I take it that Matt isn't with you tonight?'

'No,' I said. 'He's across in Orkney with Freya's family for a few days.'

'Any chance you can get Morag on the ferry and join him? I'm not happy about you being anywhere near Malcolm Goddard on your own.'

'I'll try,' I said. 'It's the holiday season so it might not be so easy to book Morag on board.'

Julie MP Adams

'Wendy,' he said. 'We both worry about Katie, but if anything happened to you, I'd never forgive myself. I mean it – look after yourself.'

Chapter 38

June 11th

As luck would have it, the ferry was booked up solid for the next two days. It would be easier, the man on the desk told me, for me to get myself to Gills and go across as a foot passenger. I was reluctant to leave Morag parked up with my few worldly goods, so I'd be loitering with intent in Caithness for the time being.

I drove to Lybster and parked on the main street, planning to take a walk down to the small harbour there. I was halfway down the hill when a Range Rover passed me, going much too fast for the single-track road, almost sending me flying down the slope. I recognised Judith Goddard's hatchet face at the wheel.

MacLean and MacLeod hadn't taken me seriously when I told them the woman was following me. Caithness, when all was said and done, is a small county and it wouldn't be unheard of to see the same people in the course of a day.

I abandoned my walk and decided to change direction. When I got back to Morag, however, I groaned. I thought I'd locked up, but when I put my hand on the door, it was open. My first thought was my bag, but I sighed with relief when I remembered I'd put my phone and wallet in my backpack. I looked down at my left hand. After I'd spoken with Kevin last night, I'd put my rings back on.

I glanced around. My jacket, which I remember draping across the bed, was now folded neatly on the front passenger seat. The tote bag I normally use as a handbag looked too tidy. If someone had been in searching, they had got it wrong. MacLeod sprung to mind, but hadn't the police been through Morag already?

I climbed out and walked round the van, checking my tyres carefully. I didn't feel safe, and I didn't trust the Goddards not to try sabotage again.

I started up the engine, and realised the broad main street came to a dead stop at the end, so I had to negotiate a six-point turn to get Morag facing the direction I was headed in. As I drove to the top of the road and made a cautious right turn, driving in the direction of Wick, I was uneasy.

My phone started ringing as I approached Thrumster, and I pulled into the forecourt of an old garage to take the call. I didn't recognise the number. I pressed the green icon to accept the call, and a woman's voice said, 'Might I speak to Wendy Latimer?'

'Speaking,' I replied.

'My name is Thalia Richards. I believe you worked for my husband?'

'Only for a day,' I replied.

'I asked your husband for your phone number,' she said.

Her voice was calm—I fully expected her to be in pieces, but her tone was determined.

'I'm sorry for your loss,' I began but she waived my sympathies aside.

'I'm in Inverness right now,' she said. 'I have to arrange

Malbister

for my husband's remains to be taken to London for his funeral, but there's a delay and I'm hiring a car to come north to Wick. Can you meet me there? I will send you a text when I arrive. I think we have some matters to discuss.'

Chapter 39

The French restaurant's décor was functional and plain, and as we'd booked at the last minute, we sat in wicker furniture in the large conservatory at the front of the building. The floor was tiled, and the walls inside part panelled in pine. The service, however, was excellent with le patron's wife, in her matelot top, bustling about with menus and the chalkboard with today's specials.

The food was the best I'd ever eaten: my smoked salmon and caper starter was utterly delicious. Across the table from me Thalia was tackling her escargot with obvious expertise. I'd worried about ordering wine, but she waved my protests away, saying that she didn't plan to start her return journey until the early evening and we had much to talk about.

She shared her sister's dark auburn colouring, and was dressed in white jeans and a sleeveless top. Her well cut navy blazer was draped on the back of her chair. There was a gold rope chain at her throat and three gold bangles on her right wrist. She wore no wedding ring. She caught me looking at her left hand.

'Joe left me two years ago,' she said. 'We were separated, but neither of us felt the need to divorce. I always thought if

Malbister

we could find Maria, we might be able to reconcile our differences and start again.'

'There's nobody else in his life?' I asked, thinking about Margaret Couper.

She lifted her glass of Merlot and took a sip, and took a piece of bread from the basket and carefully spread it with butter. 'Joe had flings all through our marriage, but he took great care to keep them from escalating to full blown affairs,' she said. 'We had an understanding.'

He was certainly attractive, I thought. Not my type though, but I took care not to say this aloud.

'You said you wanted to discuss something?' I asked.

'When my sister went missing, it destroyed our family. My parents both went to their graves not knowing what happened to her. It put a strain on our marriage, and I had to fight Goddard to stop him taking over our family business. He's evil, Mrs Latimer.'

'Call me Wendy, please.' I felt a rush of sympathy for Thalia—my family were already feeling the effect of Goddard malice.

'I've come to Scotland to bury Joe, but I want the truth too. The last message I had from him was that he was going to rescue your sister. Now, why would he want to help a woman he'd never met?'

Our second course arrived: seabass for Thalia and lamb in a café crème sauce for me. The patron's wife returned with a dish of dauphinoise potatoes, another of frites and two side dishes of perfectly steamed vegetables. For the first time in weeks, I tasted my food and was distracted by the beautiful sauce. Thalia, on the other hand, was toying with her fish. Not as cool as she made out : her hand shook as she plied her fork.

'Tell me about your sister?' I asked. I felt insensitive for enjoying my meal so much.

'Maria was my twin sister,' she said.

Of course, twins tend to run in families, don't they?

'When we were young, we could read each other's minds. We are identical twins, and they say that identical twins have a strong bond with one another. I thought we did, but there were differences too.'

'Maria was beautiful and very feminine. I was more of a tomboy, in many ways. I met Joe at a go karting event, when we both tried to get into motor racing. I knew him from my teens and we married young. Maria was much more vulnerable than me. She was working for our family business during a university vacation when she was raped. The young man was from a very wealthy, powerful family and he had the case thrown out of court. Of course, he could—his family could afford the best lawyers in Italy. Overnight, she went from being a confident young woman to a fearful child with severe anxiety. She dropped out of her degree and spent the next ten years in therapy.'

I listened intently, sipping my wine. I could recognise Kate in her description of Maria Gambini. Feminine, vulnerable, and someone who found relationships with men difficult.

'My sister was easily bullied,' I said. 'I don't think she was assaulted, but she changed jobs to avoid her bosses coming on to her.'

She nodded and took a forkful of potato, chewed and swallowed.

Le Patron, in his chef's whites approached the diners. When he came to our table, I said, truthfully that my meal was the best I had ever tasted. He smiled and thanked us, but Thalia was still only halfway through her plate. I helped myself to her frites and took another sip of the wine.

Malbister

'Our family business is in luxury goods, and we have boutiques in the resorts around Europe,' she continued. 'Papa thought it would do her good to have some responsibility and arranged for her to cover the Klosters store, while the manager there was on holiday. That was where she met Goddard. He cursed the day he let her go there.'

'Wasn't it less than a year after his first wife died? And in the same resort?' Goddard was a cold fish, alright, but returning to the scene of a tragedy within the year?

Thalia loaded a fork with her now cold seabass and steamed vegetables and chewed carefully. I was polishing off the frites as if I hadn't just enjoyed the best meal of my life. And as if I wasn't worried sick about my own sister.

'And for the death of the first wife to have been caused by his own mother? Utterly heartless,' she said.

'What?'

'Oh yes,' she said. 'Judith Goddard was the skier who crashed into Fiona. And she's the reason why we've never found out what happened to Maria.'

If looks could kill, I reckoned I would have been dead ten times over, since I first set eyes on Judith Goddard. And until this week, I'd never set eyes on the woman in person.

'She's been stalking me,' I said. I explained about the call, and about my dash north, and about how, without my knowledge, Katie told my husband that she was in fear for her life. Explaining about my 'chance' meetings with Joe, sounded far-fetched even to me. I told her about Judith and Jack Goddard menacing the people at the sales pitch, and about the twins slashing my bicycle tyres.

'I'm worried that somehow they've been able to track me since I arrived in this wretched county,' I said. 'Everywhere I go, they seem to know in advance and they are there as if by magic.'

'Sorcery, in the case of Judith Goddard,' Thalia said.

'I half expect to see her turn up here,' I said – and wondered if her absence was the reason why I was able to eat.

We were offered the dessert menu, which Thalia declined, and ordered coffee instead. I'd seen my favourite: Crème Brulee and was tempted. When the coffees arrived, I apologised to Thalia and ordered the pudding, which arrived shortly afterwards with a tantalising crisp caramel top.

'I knew a little about Joe's new project,' she explained. 'He worked for a while on a project designing yacht interiors, that Gambini's were also involved with. Maria was interning on the sales side, and they got to know one another a bit better. His passion was always design.' she said, shaking her head. 'He was useless at business, and sometimes took on investors who landed him in trouble. He spent a year in an open prison for fraud, thanks to one of them.'

I dug my spoon into my pudding, savouring each creamy mouthful, and feeling guilty about loving my food so much.

'My husband and his team are building the prototype,' I said. 'I only found out about that yesterday. Kevin couldn't get away, so Joe followed me north. I can't understand why he went to Malbister in the middle of the night? The place was full of Arabs and their security, and the story the police told me was that he got in, triggered alarms and was hit by a stray bullet. It sounds far-fetched to me,' I said.

'Tell me, 'she began, 'did you get to see your sister at all?'

I nodded. 'Only for a few minutes and she couldn't wait to get rid of me. She said something about her husband fetching his guests from the airport. I got the feeling that she'd been forced to get me to go. And she was scared.' In fact, the only time I'd seen her scared like that was in

Malbister

childhood, when she was being bullied and didn't want Dad to find out, in case he made it worse.

'So, do you think she would have wanted Joe to come storming in, making a fuss?' Thalia asked.

'I'd have said the opposite. She'd have wanted to wait. That's what she usually did.' Katie's way was always to wait until things had calmed down before telling anyone what had happened. So why did she tell Kevin before calling me? And could she have called Joe Ricci, whom she had never met, to get him to come and rescue her?'

A chill went up my spine. What if Judith had taken Katie's phone and sent a text? It sounded like a trap had been set. And knowing the Goddards – even if only for a short time – I wouldn't put it past them.

Chapter 40

We finished our coffee and Thalia paid the bill with a gold credit card, fishing out a banknote from a Gucci wallet for the tip. We only had a glass of wine each, but to be on the safe side, we went for a walk after our meal, heading across the bridge and into the part of the town called Pulteney. It was designed by Thomas Telford in the shape of a boat, with Ebenezer Street as its prow.

Passing the Black Stairs, we saw a poignant memorial garden to children killed in the first civilian bombing of the Second World War, and the Heritage Centre, where Annie Swanson told me she volunteered.

We walked past the decorative salt gates on the former fish store arches and climbed the steep Harbour Terrace to look out over the harbour. There was a marina with yachts and pleasure boats, and we saw a boat taking tourists dolphin watching, but most of the activity going on was related to the vast wind farm, off shore.

We talked of our sisters, and their weddings and our mothers, as we walked. I had the feeling that keeping busy was helping her to deal with the loss of Joe. I doubted I could be as strong.

Malbister

We returned to the car park at the Camps, on our way to a café which Annie had recommended. Suddenly my appetite vanished. I had locked Morag, when I went across to the restaurant. My motorhome was gone.

I called the police on Thalia's phone and within twenty minutes, a marked police car arrived at the car park. The middle-aged police officer, a bluff man with a beard, seemed to find the theft of my home amusing, until the female officer with him, shot him a filthy look. 'There's been a flood of motor homes since the NC500 started, and not all of them have sensible drivers. Most are hired in Inverness by folk who've never driven one before.' she explained. 'Some of the local folk's patience is wearing thin. That's not the case with you, mind,' she said as she took down the details.

When I gave the registration details and she radioed them in to her HQ, she had a rapid message on the radio. 'Mrs Latimer?' she said. 'DCI MacLeod says you've been helping with some enquiries. She says she's going to call you direct in a few minutes. Do you have your phone on you?'

I checked my handbag, only to recall I'd put the phone on the charger in Morag, and forgotten to take it off.

'My phone was in the van,' I said, feeling suddenly lightheaded.

'It's okay, Mrs Latimer. DCI MacLeod will put out an all-points bulletin on your van. They're bound to locate it soon.'

Her partner gave a guffaw. 'Aye, if it's joy riders, they usually dump vehicles once they've had their fun. A bit more complicated if its travelling folk—they swap plates and sell them on.'

The female officer said, 'I'm sure that's not going to happen with your van. We'll keep looking for her. Have you got somewhere to stay tonight?'

I shook my head. 'My sister's gone missing, and she was

the only place I could get a bed for the night. Her husband's family are hostile to me – and to Mrs Ricci here.'

A thought struck me. 'My van was broken into yesterday, in Lybster. I saw Judith Goddard nearby. Do you think she might have taken it?' To my dismay I remembered how adeptly Gussie had broken into my sister's vanity case, and her light-fingered ways. There were spare keys for Morag's ignition in the glove compartment.

'Could you check if Morag, my van, is at Malbister?'

They exchanged a look. 'It's not as simple as that. Malbister is still locked down by the security services. You'd be lucky to get anywhere near the place, and even if you did, if you tried to take your property back, you'd actually be the one in trouble. Your best chance is if the DCI comes back up with a warrant to search for it. In the meantime, I'll give you a crime number for your insurance claim. He returned to the car to fetch a printed form, and scribbled in my details.

They were gone within minutes.

Chapter 41

Thalia drove up to the gates of Malbister and I got out and pressed the intercom buzzer. There was no response. The gates remained not only closed, but chained and padlocked.

'Look, you don't have to hang around for me,' I said, trying to sound upbeat and positive. 'I can skirt around the estate and see if there's a gap in the fence. I'm pretty sure my van is in there, and if I can get into it, at least I'll have a bed for the night. You don't want to miss your flight.'

She looked doubtful. 'I don't like the idea of leaving you anywhere near this place,' she said. She reached into the back seat for her bag and pulled out a business card. 'If you need me to come back up, call the mobile number on here. Good luck.'

It was mid-afternoon, and what passed for warm in Caithness. I'd felt positively scruffy beside Thalia at lunch, but my cargo trousers and Skechers meant I was adequately dressed for exploring in the countryside.

The high walls and tall gates continued at least four miles to the west, but gave way at first to an electrified fence, which I didn't dare touch, with its symbols and warning text. Another few miles later, the firm ground turned to peat bog, and I slipped, messing up my clothes and shoes, swearing under my breath.

I heard laughter, and turned round to see a man cutting peat. He was tall and lean, and bare chested. 'I guess you're no from round here?' he said. 'I didna' mean til laugh at 'ye. If you're looking for a way into the estate, if you keep on going a wee bit further, the electric fence runs out and there's bushes. There are a few spaces where the twins sneak out. You should be able to wriggle in through there.'

I thanked him. 'Do you work on the estate?' I worried that he might be sending me into a trap.

He shook his head. 'No – and I wouldn't even if they begged me. I used to work there when it was 'e big hoose ower yonder—when it was the old factor who was in charge, but the first thing Mister Goddard did was to fire McAllister and everyone who worked with him. Said he wanted to run things differently. Be my guest.'

'Thanks again,' I said. 'What was the big house like before?'

He snorted. 'Much better than that monstrosity,' he said. 'The proportions of the new place are all wrong. And he planted trees after SNH told him not to. He's no' very popular round here.'

I continued on for about half an hour, and as the stranger had said, the electric fence petered out, replaced by a thick hedgerow. I kept my eyes peeled until I saw the gap in the fence. The twins were both pretty skinny, but I reckoned I could manage to shimmy my way through. I just hoped there weren't any guard dogs loose. And mentally I included Mrs Judith Goddard.

Once inside, I found myself on peat, but from what I could see, there was the beginnings of cultivated land ahead. I made my way cautiously, glad my clothing blended in with

Malbister

the countryside. I hoped, if the gates were locked and bolted that there wasn't going to be any shooting going on. It wasn't August 12th, I reassured myself. The police said the foreign visitors left, so with any luck, Goddard and his wretched family might not be at home. If Morag wasn't there, I might be able to nose around and see if there were any clues as to what happened to Katie.

At the back of my mind, I couldn't help thinking my actions smacked of my own favourite childhood reading – Enid Blyton's Famous Five, or Five Find Outers and Dog. I crouched down behind a drystone dyke and peeped across at the two Malbister Houses.

The peat cutter was absolutely right. The new building—the one where I'd been interrogated by McLean and MacLeod—was all wrong. The proportions reminded me of a programme I'd seen on television about Albert Speer. Kevin had been really excited by it, pointing out that the oversized pillars were deliberate, as a way of disorienting people, pulling them into the Nazis' hideous attempt to be the Roman Empire. It was a statement – and Goddard's was that he was prepared to break any rules to get his own way. I wondered how on earth he'd got planning permission for something so big and brutalist.

The old house, in contrast, roofless and burned out as it was, had a charm, similar to the place in Monarch of the Glen, my Mum's favourite Sunday night viewing years ago. The sandstone building had graceful turrets and gables, and although it was no older than Victorian, the faux battlements gave it the look of a much older building.

I skirted round the new building, almost losing my footing and looking down at the sheer drop below, a couple of times. I drew a deep breath when I reached the outbuildings of the old house. There was a barn, and a stable with loose boxes. I heard barking from the nearby kennels, but thankfully the dogs were secure behind bars and whoever was looking after them didn't appear to be nearby.

I edged into the barn, and there, to my relief was Morag. Someone had let the air out of her tyres, but hopefully I'd be able to do something about that. I just hoped my phone was still inside. I fumbled in my bag for my keys and let myself in.

There was no sign of my phone. At least, now, I had a bed for the night, and I'd eaten well at lunch, so I wasn't going to starve. I climbed out and decided to explore the rest of the outbuildings.

There was tack for two ponies in the stables, and in the paddock behind, I saw the twins' two mounts. Katie's Audi was in the garage, but there was no sign of the two Range Rovers, which was a relief.

As I reached the end of the row of buildings, I heard a frantic tapping. The last building was an old cottage with a heavy bolt on the door. A voice frantically called my name. I looked through the dirty window at my sister.

Chapter 42

I struggled with the rusted bolt on the door, but finally tugged it open and Katie rushed into my arms. She was frantically speaking nineteen to the dozen, and nothing she said appeared to make any sense.

'Slow down,' I said. 'Start from the beginning.'

I pulled her into the sunlight. The cottage behind her had dirty walls which at one point must have been painted white. There was a single bed with a tartan rug on it, and on a table under the dirty window was an old-fashioned jug and basin. It had the look of a prison. I'd seen Katie only a few days before, but already she had the pallor of a prisoner. The dark circles below her eyes showed she hadn't slept.

'Blimey, Kate. What in hell's name is going on?'

'Where do I start?' she sobbed.

A dry voice behind us said 'You'll have plenty of time for that.'

Jack Goddard stood behind us. In one hand was my old iPhone and in the other was a baseball bat.

I woke with a thumping headache. I was stretched out on the bed in the cottage, and Kate was slumped against the door, sitting on the floor with her head on her knees. I tried to sit up, but the cramp in my left arm was due to my left wrist being handcuffed to the bed. Outside the window it was almost dark. I'd been out of it for hours.

Kate was also handcuffed.

I coughed and she looked up, dull eyed and in obvious pain. Jack Goddard was pretty handy with that bat. I suspected if we got out, we'd need to be checked over in a hospital.

'Kate,' I croaked. My mouth was dry. 'Any chance you can reach that water glass?'

She struggled to her feet and lifted the half empty glass of stale water, shuffling towards the bed to hold it out to me. I took it in my free hand and raised it to my lips.

'What's going on, Katie? Why are we in here?'

She sat down awkwardly on the bed. 'I'm scared, Wendy. Don't think I'm not glad to see you – I am. But you've walked into a trap. They've got something horrible planned for us – but I don't know what it is yet.'

'Why? Is this down to your husband?' I asked.

She was white faced and shaking. 'I don't know. I found something out about this place shortly after we moved here. I kept it to myself—I wish I hadn't now. Mum was dead and Dad was packing up to move away. I'd come down with Malcolm to go to the theatre, one of his corporate do's where he'd taken a box at the Opera, and I'd taken the train down to see Dad. I was walking back to the station when I met Kevin. He saw I was upset about something, and he took me for a drink and I blurted out that I didn't feel safe.'

'What was all of that business with the burner phone?' I asked.

Her eyes flew open wide. 'Oh God,' she whispered. 'They don't know about that, do they?'

I nodded. 'Do you want the rest of this water?' She took

Malbister

the glass between her hands and drained it thirstily.

'Kevin asked if I had an old phone, and he bought me a SIM card to go into it. He came up with some codes and said if I was really scared, he would find a way to get the police to come and get me. I hid it away safely, and I checked in with him. How do you know they found it?'

'I visited with Matt, the day before yesterday, looking for you,' I said. 'The twins knew about it and one of them broke into your little case and produced it. The police have it now.'

She looked at me blankly. 'The police?'

'Yes,' I said. 'They were investigating the murder of Kevin's boss, Joe. I had lunch with his widow today.'

'Joe?' she repeated.

'Yes,' I said. I wondered if she was concussed. She didn't seem to be taking anything in. 'Joe Ricci was shot by the security men who were here with the Middle East guests. The ones you were worried about my seeing?'

'Why was he here?' she asked.

'That's one of the things I was trying to find out,' I said. My left ankle was itchy. Goodness knows what could have bitten me when I was stumbling in and out of the peat bog yesterday. I wanted to scratch, but I couldn't quite reach. 'Kevin's been working for Joe Ricci, building a prototype holiday tiny house. After your alert came in, Joe told Kevin, and he said he would come north to check on you. Kevin got him to follow me up here, and we kept meeting by accident. He and his wife have been trying to find out what happened to her sister—the second wife your husband had declared legally dead.

'I was working for Joe Ricci, as a temp,' I said. 'I thought I could cover the cost of the petrol for getting here. Jack and your mother-in-law came to the meeting and intimidated the folk who were thinking of buying holiday lodges for their crofts. I was supposed to be working at a sales pitch the day after, and I saw his car at Dunnet Head – but he wasn't with it. I told the police after he didn't turn up at the next venue.'

'Then, when Matt and I came here, Matt and Freya – his girlfriend – walked down to look at the broch, and they found Joe's body. He'd been shot. The police got warned off by the Home Office – it seems your guests were the sort who can nip in and out of the country and claim diplomatic immunity.'

She looked puzzled. 'Is that what he told them? Mr Shaikh is a banker—he brought his son with him, but he's not a diplomat, and they didn't have any security guards.'

'If there were no foreign assassins, what happened?' I asked.

'I honestly don't know,' she replied.

'Okay, so let's cut to the chase,' I suggested. 'What exactly did you find out that got you scared enough to get into cahoots with Kev?'

She looked offended, and for a moment I saw the child she had been, full of affronted dignity, like a cat that falls off a window ledge.

'Malcolm has an explanation for everything,' she began. 'To begin with, he was perfect: kind, loving, attentive – but little by little, he took everything away from me. First it was the cats—he said one of his daughters was severely allergic—so I got Betsy to take them, and she sublet my flat. Then, he said he didn't want me to go on working in London when we were moving up here, so I arranged at first to work from home, and then we had issues with our internet and phone.'

'So?' I asked, 'was he telling the truth?'

'The girls aren't allergic. You've seen them with the dogs, and they spend a lot of time riding. That was a fib, and I should have cottoned on to it earlier. I found out he was

Malbister

switching the phones and the internet off at a master switch in his office. I was being gaslighted out of my job.'

Good, I thought. At least she knew what he was up to.

'So, what scared you?' I asked, gently.

'Katie, I think Judith killed his first two wives. And I think she's trying to get rid of me.'

Chapter 43

The day passed slowly. I was bursting for the loo, and being chained to the bed meant I was stuck. Katie indicated an ancient chamber pot under the bed and I manoeuvred myself to a position where I could squat. She turned her face to the window to spare my embarrassment. I emptied my bladder, but my bowels were loose, and we would have to put up with the awful smell.

The only indicator of time was the shadows on the wall. It was almost the summer solstice, so even the shifting light was no reliable indicator of time.

We were being held against our will. Wasn't wrongful imprisonment a crime? Suddenly, living in Morag, where at least I had a bathroom of sorts and clean bedding, felt like luxury. The cottage had been used as a wood store, and there were some logs still piled in a corner. Every so often I saw a movement from the corner of my eye. I was convinced there was a rat behind the logs, and I shivered.

Our phones were gone and we had no way of making contact with the outside world. Katie drifted in and out of sleep in her hunched position on the floor. I felt my head—there was a bump the size of an egg on the back of my skull.

Malbister

Katie must have taken the blows on her shoulder, because she kept trying to raise her manacled hands to feel it, but screwing up her face in pain and dropping her hands back on her knees. I worried that I had a cracked skull and my sister had a fracture.

There was no water left and my mouth was too parched to speak. I wondered if the inhabitants of the house had simply cleared off and left us to die. Was that what they'd done to Maria Gambini? Locked her up somewhere and left her to die?

Who knew I was here? I wish I'd had the presence of mind to call Matt, when Morag was stolen. Then at least someone would have an idea of where to look for me. I knew he was in love with Freya—he had the same dopey look that Kevin had when we were Matt's age. His mum wasn't likely to be high on his list of priorities. Besides, I'd worked out that the Goddards were plausible liars. If he did contact them, they'd no doubt be able to fob him off?

I wondered, too, what Kevin would be thinking. I hoped he wouldn't do anything rash that would see him killed too.

My head hurt like mad, and I was dehydrated which made the pain worse. You can live for days without food, but to be left hours on end without water is dangerous.

I had no idea of the time when we heard the bolt being drawn back. One of the twins ushered in a thin man, with a supermarket carrier bag and a bucket. He removed the stinking chamber pot, leaving the bucket, which reeked of portaloo chemicals, in its place. The twin made a disgusted face as he passed her at the door. She slammed the door shut, shoving the bolt back into place.

I reached for the bag. Inside was a two-litre bottle of water, paper cups and two packets of supermarket sandwiches. 'Hardly the Ritz,' I said. 'Who was that man,

Katie?'

'He's one of the estate workers. Malcolm fell out with the locals and he hired some Albanians. They don't speak any English.'

Goddard had everything worked out. Nobody we could appeal to for help—if the person who brought us food and water couldn't speak our language. I wondered about trying to slip him a note, but my bag was gone. I couldn't see any writing tools in our prison.

Katie struggled to her knees to get water and her sandwich, but her arm must be broken. She struggled to open the bottle and I was scared she would drop it and our precious water would spill on the packed earth floor. 'Give it here,' I said. I wedged the bottle between my knees and slowly managed to turn the top single handed. It wasn't sealed, which worried me, but I was too thirsty to care. Somehow, I managed to pour a cup for each of us. After a few sips, my mouth was sufficiently moist to speak.

'Katie, when did they shut you in here?' I asked.

She was disorientated, and weak, and I doubted she knew which day it was, but she replied. 'The same day that you came to the house. Malcolm had dinner in the office wing with the Shaikhs and told the rest of us to stay in the other side. Jack and the twins went outside, and I saw my car being driven off. He's not on my insurance, and he takes the keys whenever it suits him.' She frowned, thinking back to that awful evening. 'I walked across to the stable block because I knew the twins had forgotten to fill the horses' water trough, and while I was in there, someone grabbed me from behind. The next thing I knew, I woke up on that bed, chained up like you are now.'

'Katie, who do you think it was that grabbed you? Was it your husband? '

Malbister

Katie isn't very tall—she's smaller than me, and always wore heels. She couldn't weigh much more than eight stones, so it wasn't beyond the possibilities for her attacker to be a woman. Judith Goddard might be in her seventies, but she was taller than Katie, and from what I saw of her, in pretty good shape for her age.

Kate shook her head. 'I think it was one of the Albanians,' she said. 'But it was Judith who put the handcuffs on me.'

I was trying to add two and two and make them come out at four, but now I was suspicious of everyone. I wondered if Joe was lured to Malbister by someone using Katie's phone. But Katie barely knew his name, let alone his phone number. As to who killed him, I wouldn't put anything past the Goddards.

And yet, Malcolm Goddard was genuinely shocked when he saw the twins had Kate's mobile. Might his concern be for real?

Chapter 44

June 12th

There was something in our drinking water, I realised, as Katie struggled to stay awake. We were being fed – just a little, and we had taken some fluids, but not enough to rehydrate our poor battered, bruised bodies. God only knows what was in the water. I suspected some sort of barbiturate, and I squinted at the bottle to see if I could find any sediment.

The lump on my head was still hard and sore, and my body ached from holding my arm at an awkward angle. The handcuff was fastened to the lower bar of the old iron bed, leaving me minimal options for movement. I was struck with cramp in my left leg and struggled to my feet to stamp my left foot on the floor, to alleviate the agony.

My mind was trying to race, but being pulled back, like a tight rein on a galloping horse. I couldn't get free of thinking about the chain of coincidences over the past week. Those chance meetings with Joe Ricci; the edited version he gave of his relationship to the Goddards ; and of course, my meeting with Thalia, his wife.

Malbister

When I sank back onto the greasy pillow and slept, I kept seeing Thalia as she handed me that card. I thought of Joe, with his generosity, buying gifts for a man he disliked and suspected. I'd seen his body in the broch – but who pulled the trigger?

The Goddards spun a line about foreign dignitaries and their security to explain away the killing, so why did the police take it seriously enough to call off the Police Scotland team? Did Goddard have an old Etonian friend in the Home Office prepared to cover his tracks?

I had one hope: DCI MacLeod knew who I was and the officers who took details of the vehicle theft were supposed to report it on to her. She was nobody's fool, and I knew she was looking for Kate. The last place anyone would think to look for a missing wife was in the grounds of her own home. On the other hand, who would be looking for me? If the gates of Malbister were locked and chained, who would get inside the grounds to find us?

If I could slip the card to the Albanian, when he returned to empty the toilet bucket and bring our next sandwich? No – he would be accompanied by one of the Goddard kids or Judith. I dreaded another encounter with Jack and his baseball bat.

I thought back to those old war movies my father-in-law was obsessed with. Every Christmas he would commandeer the telly to watch The Great Escape. What would one of those heroes do? What would the Famous Five do for that matter? I looked around for something to pick the lock on my handcuffs. I needed a hairgrip or a nail, but looking round, I could see nothing. I thought of how adept that twin was in opening other people's private property: a vanity case or a motorhome. I wondered who taught her those skills.

Later in the day, I managed to gather my wits sufficiently

to ask Kate when she began to suspect Judith Goddard of killing Fiona and Maria.

'It was the cap,' she said. 'I found the cap Maria was wearing when she vanished.'

The newspapers and Crimewatch showed stills from the CCTV cameras that tracked Maria Goddard from the family home to the railway station. Her long auburn hair was tucked up into a tweed Baker Boy cap, and she wore a knee length black coat over black jeans and ankle boots. A pashmina was wound round her neck. She carried a capacious handbag and she looked as if she was trying to be inconspicuous. The police pored over the footage and compared the tall slender woman with the people who got off the train at each station. Each station but two – where the cameras were out of service. They'd searched the cameras on the roads around each of those stations, but the woman in the cap had vanished into thin air.

When the Goddard house in London was packed up, ahead of the move to Malbister, Kate realised she'd packed her hairdryer away and walked through to Judith's rooms to borrow hers. Judith was outside, directing the removal men, and Kate opened the wardrobe door. Among Judith's clothes, there was a basket of odds and ends, with the hairdryer on top. She lifted it up, intending to take it to the hall socket to plug it in, but as she did so, she saw the cap, scrunched up.

It didn't at first register. Kate was simply borrowing a common or garden item. However, Kate had never seen her mother-in-law wear a hat of any sort. As she was returning the dryer to the wardrobe, Judith strode in, a look of utter fury on her face and struck Kate hard, on both cheeks.

'She was an utter harpy,' Kate said. 'I was used to her bossing me; bossing Malcolm for that matter – but I'd never

Malbister

seen her lose her temper like that. She accused me of going through her things; of invading her privacy. If looks could kill, I would have dropped down dead on the spot.'

'I knew that she knew I'd seen the cap. And when she walked down the stairs, I realised the girl on that train wasn't Maria—it was her.'

It sounded far-fetched, but it wasn't impossible. Judith could easily have dressed in her daughter in law's clothing, left the house and headed for the station, then slipped off at one of those stations, changed clothes, and returned home as her much older self. What had she done with Maria Gambini? And what did she have in store for Maria's successor, and for me?

We needed to get out of here, before she had the time to put those plans into action.

Chapter 45

A fortnight ago, I was a soon to be redundant junior manager in a department store, about to be homeless, with a failing marriage. I didn't realise how lucky I was. I wasn't worried about my sister. I had my two kids, my motorhome and a summer of drifting and temping ahead of me. There was nobody trying to kill me, and I had my health and my freedom.

Now, I was imprisoned in a cottage that was more like a cell, chained to a bed and drugged into compliance. The Goddards were out to kill us—I was sure of that. All they'd need to do was leave us here to die. If that main gate was chained up, what was to stop them?

I was terrified for Kate—she was lying on the blanket, with her head on the pillow. I'd chucked the pillow and blanket off the bed and was lying on the ticking cover of the mattress, trying not to think of bedbugs that might be lurking in it. I attempted sitting up, and my head swam.

Eventually, I managed to scramble into a sitting position. From what I could make out, it was now late afternoon. We had slept most of the day—whatever they put into our water was having the intended effect.

Malbister

I'd peered round looking for a nail, or pin – anything to try to pick the lock of my handcuffs. Now I realised the bed was a basic one. I'd thought it was as old as the cottage, but I felt it wobble and suspected it was held together with bolts. If I could get one of the bolts loose, I might be able to free myself. I couldn't sit here doing nothing.

I needed to use that bucket, so I struggled to my feet and straddled it, feeling the relief of passing water. I worried about kidney damage—sooner or later I was going to need to drink the drugged water, if only to restore my fluids.

I finished with the bucket, pushing it to the side and knelt down beside the bed. I was right about the side struts being held with bolts, and to my relief, they were the type with a large screw head rather than the sort that required an Allen key. I searched my trouser pockets for a coin, and found a penny. I hoped that our captors wouldn't feel the need to come and tell us a bedtime story – at least not before I had freed myself and had some sort of weapon to hand.

The process was long and time consuming. Umpteen times, I dropped the coin and had to scrabble on the ground to retrieve it. One by one, I managed to free the bolts and dropped them on the floor.

The stable block and this cottage were much older than the original Malbister House. At some point, two hundred years ago, the original occupants were given their marching orders and their home – their croft – was taken over by a bunch of toffee-nosed aristocrats who turned it into outhouses for their hunting lodge. Whereas the older Malbister House had sprung wooden floors, high ceilings and bay windows; the cottage floor was made of hard packed earth. I wondered how deep the foundations were, and thinking of the Great Escape, I wondered if we'd be able to dig our way out.

Julie MP Adams

It was the butterfly that made me look up. It was pale and creamy in colour with a feathered pattern on its wings. I'd not seen it earlier – but now, it drew my gaze to the low ceiling. It was made of planks, and there was a hatch. I racked my brains to remember the barn next door to it. Above the loose boxes was an open hay barn. If I could free myself from the bed, I could try to open the hatch and crawl through the roof space to the barn. Hopefully that would let me open the bolt on the cottage door and we could try to escape. I'd freed the side rail from the bed, but needed to remove the springs in the base to slide the handcuffs free. It was a tricky process and I had to avoid being scratched by the rusty springs. I wondered if my tetanus was up to date, before remembering it was the least of my worries. Finally, I freed the cuff from the bed. I checked outside the window – but the stable yard alley was deserted.

I pulled the stool in the corner closer to the hatch and tentatively stood on it, feeling it wobble a bit. I had to bend my neck—the roof was only seven feet high, and I'm five foot eight. I drew the bolt on the roof hatch and pushed it up.

I looked back at Katie, and climbed down to kneel beside her. I put a hand on her forehead. She was burning up. I didn't dare try to give her any of the drugged water. 'Hold on, Katie,' I said, 'I'm going to try and get us out of here. '

My tomboy childhood came in handy as I grabbed the edge of the hatch and pushed my elbows on to the loft floor. I gave a hop and brought my knees up and wriggled on my belly into the loft. It was dusty and I saw something scurry into a corner. Once up there, I lowered the hatch and squinted. There was no natural light, but I calculated the distance to the start of the loose boxes, and crawled towards it. There was no wall, only a curtain of sacking, which opened

Malbister

out into the open rafters of the hayloft. The loose boxes were empty: the ponies were out in the field. I lowered myself to the stone floor, landing awkwardly.

Looking out of the open door, to see if there were signs of movement and finding none, I reached down, slid the bolt, to let myself out, and edged along the alley to slide the bolt on our prison.

Chapter 46

Katie looked awful. I raised her to her feet, trying to avoid causing any further hurt to her poor arm. I'd need to get us out of here, but first, I needed to get us some water. Morag was in the barn, and if I could get Katie in there, I could at least make her comfortable and get some liquids into both of us, while I worked out what to do next.

I felt in my pocket for my van key, and half carried Kate along the alley. The new house didn't have a direct view of the alley, thankfully. The barn door was open, and the other vehicles were missing. I helped my sister to lean on the barn wall while I prowled round Morag, to see if there were any booby traps laid for us. I didn't trust the Goddards not to have cut the brakes or sabotaged more than the tyres.

We climbed in, and I fished in the cupboards for a soft drink can. I pulled the ring and held it to Katie's lips. She drank thirstily and shot me a rueful smile. 'Thanks, Wendy.'

I found some snacks and opened a packet of crisps, then realising the pain she was in, I fed them to her one by one. All the while I was calculating how I was going to get us out of here. No way would she cope with having to take the path behind the new house and into the bushes. She was far too

Malbister

weak. I turned the dining area back into a double bed and made her lie down to rest.

How long would it be until the Albanian returned with the next toilet bucket and food? And how long before we were returned to our grim little cell?

I opened another can and drank it, while my mind raced nineteen to the dozen. I had no phone and if I was going to get us out of here, we had two options. One was for me to try and get the air back into Morag's tyres and see if we could get out through the gates. I remembered the chains and the padlock. While Kate knew the code to open the gates, we'd have to ram them to break those chains.

The only other plan was for me to try to get out of the estate the way I'd come in, and raise the alarm. If I could get to the nearest house, I could call the police. The question was, how long could Kate be left without medical help?

I felt my own head. My bump was less like an egg, but still sore to the touch.

Thankfully, we owned a compressor. After we'd had a flat tyre and a flat spare wheel, Kevin had insisted on having one. I climbed out and crouching low, I reinflated the tyres. They'd been carefully deflated and not slashed, which was one thing to be grateful for. I climbed back into the van afterwards and checked on Katie. I intended to wait until it was dark—by the looks of it, it was already about eleven at night, then start the van and get it to the gates.

'Kate, what's the code for the gate?'

She looked at me blankly. 'They change the code every day. It's a random thing to stop anyone giving it away.'

'Do you think we'd be able to ram the gates, if I drive at them fast?'

She shook her head. 'Malcolm had them made of reinforced steel. All you'd do would write the van off.'

Plan B it would need to be, then.

I made Kate as comfortable as I could, inside Morag. I'd bathed her face with lukewarm water, and placed a cold facecloth on her fevered brow. She was groaning with pain, but I'd managed to find some paracetamol in my first aid box, and given her two caplets. I gave myself a perfunctory wash and changed into a black t shirt and jeans, pulling a black buff over my hair and lacing up my baseball boots, hoping I'd blend into the late dusk of June. I looked like a cat burglar. I didn't feel like one. My heart was pumping frantically and I was scared stiff of failure.

I slipped noiselessly out of Morag, closing the driver's side door as quietly as I could, and looked around the barn, before sidling to the doors and glancing out. I had to ensure I stayed downwind from the kennels, to avoid the dogs picking up my scent and barking to raise the alarm.

In order for my plan to work, I needed to pick up the path at the back of the stable block and drop to my knees to stay out of sight of the new Malbister House. Then I'd need to skirt the edge of the fields and head for the gap in the hedge. The light was fading, but it was not quite dark yet. As I skirted the side of the barn, I could see three vehicles parked in the middle of the yard that separated the Old Malbister Lodge from the new building: both Range Rovers and Kate's Audi A1. If they were all indoors, would I have been better off trying to ram the gates and get Kate to hospital?

I reached the drystone dyke and dropped to a crouch. I risked a quick look up at the windows, but fortunately there didn't appear to be anyone at the back of the house. I followed the path I'd taken yesterday, bypassing the stand of trees and the broch, and stayed close to the hedgerows at the edge of the fields, trying to blend into the darkness.

Malbister

I heard voices speaking in a language I didn't understand and I flattened myself to the ground. There were two men and they appeared to be arguing over something. I just hoped they weren't going to be dropping in to our prison. I'd taken care to bolt the door and shoved the pillow under the blanket, to try and look as if someone was hunched up in sleep. 'Please,' I prayed to no one in particular, 'Don't go into the barn.'

After what seemed like hours, but could only have been about forty minutes or so, I shimmied through the hedge and was on the peat land outside the walls of Malbister.

By the time I stumbled through the wet ground, keeping close to the scary electric fence, and reached the outside of the gates, it was actually dark. The sun had dipped, and I could make out some stars. In just over a week, it would be the Solstice. Annie Swanson said when she was a school pupil, there was a tradition of climbing Morven – a mountain in the distance – to watch the sun set and rise again.

I made my way down the single-track road and finally reached the A99. It was going to be a long walk to Wick.

Chapter 47

June 13th

The logical thing to do, I reasoned, would be to try to walk to Wick on the A99. The A9 splits at Latheron and continues to Thurso, while the A99 goes through Wick and joins a smaller road to get to Groats. If I was lucky, I might be able to hitch a lift to get to the town. However, I worried that if anyone had gone into the old cottage, and realised we were missing, the first thing they'd do would be to send a vehicle on the road to pick me up. If I was picked up on the main road, I would be taking a risk. It was safer to walk all night, if necessary. When I reached Thrumster, I took a left onto a side road, that I guessed would take me in on the other side of the town, and might also give me a hiding spot. I cursed the loss of my phone. The public phone boxes all seemed to have vanished, now, so finding one to call 999 was out of the question.

My best hope was to get to the police station in Wick and ask for help there.

My choice of road added miles to my walk, but I'd slept so long the previous day, I had a sort of second wind. My

Malbister

head still hurt and I worried about being able to walk the distance without coming to grief. I'd shoved the packet of fruit gums I always kept in the driver side door rack into the pocket of my jeans and rationed myself to one sweet every mile or so, to keep my energy levels up. The handcuffs were still on my left hand and I felt their weight rub at my wrist. The only relief came from either holding them in my hand, which gave me cramp, or putting them in my jeans pocket, but somehow, it affected my balance as I walked and I had to let them dangle.

I walked past crofts, and farmhouses, and new build bungalows with pick-ups and SUV's in their gravelled driveways. I saw barns with electric doors keeping tractors safe from rural robbers. I woke up a dog at one place—he set up a loud barking that sounded anything but friendly. Nobody stirred. Once away from the immediate area of Malbister, I could just as easily knock on a door and ask for the use of a phone, but I'd grown suspicious, and I needed the police to believe me and go and get Kate to hospital. Besides, who would open the door to a wild-eyed woman like me? I'd attempted to tidy myself up, but I must look a fright.

Away from the main road, the ground was mainly rough grazing, and there were flocks of sheep and an occasional goat in the fields. One croft had a shed with one side of chicken wire, though which I could see the woolly pom-pom heads of a herd of alpacas.

The sun rose from the horizon as I walked, and taking short breaks, sitting on the ground, in between walking, I reached Newton Woods, at the top of a long straight road which led directly to the police station, at six in the morning. There were birds singing and the closer I got to Wick, the gulls wheeled overhead. My poor feet were blistered and sore, and I was light headed after my long walk. With the dawn I saw farmers coming out to check on their livestock and some people returning home from night shift work.

I looked down the hill at the town, with Pulteney's distinctive grid pattern of Georgian streets, and the spire of the Parish Church across the river, and sighed. I popped the last fruit gum in my mouth and set off down the hill.

I passed the newly built school campus on my right. There were ponies in the field to my left, and they raised their heads from cropping the grass to look at me. It all looked so lovely and normal. I could understand why people did the NC500, but right now, I wanted to be at the other end of Britain. I wished Kate never set eyes on Goddard, let alone marry him.

At the foot of the hill, I walked down Newton Road, with its tidy gardens and neat wrought iron fences, crossed Thurso Street and within my sight was the railway station and Police Station. I took a deep breath and crossed to ring the bell.

My heart sank when I saw the notice on the door which said it didn't open until 8am. The train station across the road was open, so I walked across and lowered myself to the ground on the platform. The first train of the day left just as I reached the station. The next one would leave just after 8. A drunk arrived, and kicked the waiting room door when he realised, he'd missed the train. He slumped down on the platform yards away from me, and slept with his head on his rucksack.

The Goddards did a real job on me. They'd locked up my motorhome—when I passed those massive gates, the chains were still wound round and padlocked. They'd locked me up—it was only by taking a huge risk that I'd escaped. They had my bag, with my purse and bank cards, and my

Malbister

remaining cash, and more important than that, they'd taken my phone, and could use it to lure the people I loved into danger. My sister was badly injured and I'd been physically attacked.

The station staff – all three of them – checked the waiting room was locked and returned to their office to brew their morning tea. The guard, a woman in her thirties, looked out and said, 'Are you alright?' I raised my head and nodded, but a few minutes later, she came out with two paper cups of tea. 'I feel guilty leaving the two of you here. Next train is going to board just after quarter to eight. '

I took the hot drink, thanking her and sipped at it gratefully. I thought of Kate, back in Malbister, in pain, and hoped that once the police station opened, that someone would believe me.

My only fear was that my absence was discovered and that the Goddards would come after me.

At quarter to eight, the engines on the second train of the day started and the lights on the doors lit up. My companion on the platform woke with a start and hoisting his rucksack, clambered onto the train. 'Are ye no' comin' on here?' he asked me. I shook my head and walked to the end of the station, where I could keep my eyes on the police station door. Minutes later, a patrol car parked and two officers got out, and shortly afterwards, a civilian in plain clothes arrived and pressed the code into the keypad. I crossed the car park and pressed the bell.

Chapter 48

'You realise that all of this sounds far-fetched, Mrs Latimer?' The officer sitting on the opposite side of the table in the interview room looked sceptical. All through last night, on my long hike, I'd rehearsed what I was going to say. Now it looked as if it was going to be me in trouble, as opposed to the Goddards.

'Yesterday, my motor home was stolen,' I repeated. 'I reported the theft to your officers and they gave me a crime number. I told them that I thought the van could have been taken to Malbister House, but they didn't want to follow that up, and they left me without my vehicle and the roof over my head.'

The officer said, 'Wait here a minute,' and left the room. It was a tiny space with no external window, painted a dark blue. It felt claustrophobic, and I was worried about Katie, lying in pain and in grave danger. Every moment spent here was wasting time. I needed to get the police to go to her rescue.

He returned with a form and a notepad. 'Right, Mrs Latimer, we have your vehicle registration and your contact telephone number. I've got someone on the desk working on your crime number at the moment.'

I thought carefully about what to say next. It was important that I stressed the police were already looking at Malbister.

'I spoke to CID after Joe Ricci was found dead in the broch at Malbister House. They told me the death was being investigated by the security services, but they were looking for my sister, who'd gone missing.'

The officer had nice hands. They were strong and square, and his fingernails were well kept. As he took notes with a Pentel on the form, he glanced at the large utility watch on his left wrist. I suspected his patience would run out soon.

'I had lunch at the French restaurant in Wick just before my van was stolen with Mrs Thalia Richards – the wife of the man who was killed. I asked her afterwards to take me to Malbister. I thought my van was there—my brother in law's family have been stalking me, and I thought if I could get into the estate, I might be able to take my property back.'

He sat back in his chair, and looked at me. His face had been open and sympathetic before, but now I saw suspicion written on every feature. I'd gone from a victim to a suspect, and I felt uncomfortable.

'So, you are saying the vehicle was taken by a relative? You do realise that invalidates any insurance claim?'

'The Goddards aren't *my* family. My sister's the wife of Malcolm Goddard. He reported her missing.' I said, firmly.

'When I arrived at the gates, and Mrs Richards left me there, I saw they were closed and chained and padlocked. I met a man cutting peat, who told me there was a way in further along the side fence, and I managed to get into the estate,' I continued.

He left the room again, and this time returned with another officer, with a laptop. The other officer said, 'The security services and the MIT instructed that the estate was to be sealed off, to protect the crime scene. There's a foreign involvement in the case—you do realise there's a news blackout over the death of Mr Ricci? And by entering the estate, you've been guilty of trespass, Mrs Latimer, as well as possibly interfering with a crime scene.'

So much for all those rights of access the NC500 booklet boasted. I pressed on. 'Once inside the estate, I located my property in the barn, and in a cottage next to the barn and the stables, I found my sister, who was being kept prisoner, and in handcuffs. I was going to help get her out, but we were assaulted by her stepson with a baseball bat. He handcuffed me to a bed, and left Kate with a broken arm.'

They looked disbelieving. To be honest, if I was on the other side of that table, I'd find my story hard to believe too.

'Look,' I said, turning my head. 'There's still a blooming great bump on my head. I'm not making this up,' I pleaded. I raised my left arm, to which the handcuffs were still attached. My wrist was chafed raw. Now I saw their expression change.

The first police officer went out of the room. 'We need to get your head looked at by the police surgeon,' the other one said, as he tapped on the laptop keypad. When the other came back into the room, he had a bunch of keys with him, and tried several before finally releasing my hand from the wretched things. I sighed with relief and rubbed my tender wrist.

'They took my phone, when they took the van, but after they hit us and locked us up, they took my bag, with all of my things – my purse and my credit cards – and they left us with water that was drugged to make us sleep.'

They were looking at one another, and I could see what they were thinking. A madwoman walks in to a police station

Malbister

and accuses a wealthy landowner of assault, theft, and false arrest?

'So, Mrs Latimer, you appear to have done a Houdini? How, exactly, did you get free?'

I explained about how I freed myself from the bolts and how I'd escaped through the loft and got Kate into the van. I told them about how I'd made my way back to the main road and walked through the night. My only hope now was that they would send someone to Malbister to locate the van and my sister, and rescue both before the Goddards had time to dispose of them.

They were still sceptical. They left the room and the doctor on duty, summoned from the hospital across the road from the police station arrived. She wore a white coat and a hijab, and she parted my hair to feel the lump on my head. Then she perched on the table beside me and shone a torch into my eyes, and asked me to touch my finger to my nose. 'Follow my finger,' she said, moving her finger to the left and to the right.

She pressed a stethoscope to my back and listened, gravely, then took my left wrist in her cool hand and felt my pulse, before looking at the marks on my wrist.

'I do not think you are concussed, Mrs Latimer, but I would suggest you take it easy for a few days. I'm concerned you might have sustained other injuries and I would like to refer you for some tests. The hospital is nearby, and we can do some of these this morning, but you might need to go to Raigmore.'

The last thing I needed was to be confined anywhere. At least not until Katie was safe.

Then they left me, alone in that room, for what felt like hours.

A third officer, a woman, came in with a cup of tea,

Julie MP Adams

which I accepted gratefully, and another form. She sat down, and asked for my emergency contact numbers, which I struggled to remember. Mobile phones have a contacts list, and who remembers numbers these days? My diary was in my bag, which my captors took from me. I rattled off the names of my husband, Kevin Latimer, who was currently working for JTC Holdings; my son, Matthew Latimer, who was currently with his girlfriend's family in Stromness. I racked my brain and remembered his mobile number. And I remembered my friend Dorothy's landline number.

The police brought in a landline handset and I called Matt. 'Mum? What's happened?'

The sound of his voice was such a relief I wanted to cry. 'I'm at the police station in Wick,' I said. 'I found your aunt, but the van was stolen, I was attacked and I managed to escape. I had to leave her behind—she was too hurt to be moved. The only thing is that I've got no phone and no purse with me. Could you ring the bank and cancel my cards for me?'

He said, 'Damn the bank cards, Mum. I'm coming across to fetch you.'

'No, darling,' I said. 'I'm safe – the police are going to help me, but I need you to ring your dad, and tell him he needs to claim on the insurance, if he can. If you can do those things for me, I'll see you soon. Aunt Kate's been hurt too, and I'm going to need to be here for her. The police surgeon wants me to go to the hospital to be checked out, so you'd only be waiting around for me.'

He said, 'I can't leave you for five minutes, Mum. Okay, but don't get into any more trouble.'

Chapter 49

Caithness General Hospital was built in the 1980s, in the days when the nuclear power plant at Dounreay was the major employer in the area. Annie Swanson said it used to be a teaching hospital for Aberdeen University, but in recent years, most of the services were centralised in Raigmore and it was being run down. The police having taken all the details of my ordeal, the female officer walked across with me to the front door of the hospital and spoke to the receptionist who sat at a vast semi-circular desk.

She, in turn, sent me to the small waiting area in the A&E reception. The police doctor wanted me to have further tests and refused to take no for an answer.

I only agreed, once the police promised to send officers to Malbister and to call DCI MacLeod.

A nurse called me through and the same doctor as before arrived and repeated the simple tests she had run before, while the nurse tended to my wrists. I was sent for an ECG and then for a CT scan to check if my skull was fractured. I had to take off my clothes and put on a hospital gown. I hoped they wouldn't insist on keeping me in, but after the scan, they put a wristband on me, and said they were keeping me in overnight for observation.

All the while, I wondered what was happening at Malbister.

Late in the afternoon, as I lay in a bed, fretting and desperately wanting to discharge myself, two police officers came to the nurses' station and spoke quietly. The nurse, brought me a dressing gown that looked as if it had seen better days and draped it over my shoulders. 'The police are here to speak to you, Wendy. They're in the family room. That's down the corridor and turn right.'

I'd not seen these two before. The man and woman introduced themselves, indicating their number on their uniforms and presenting their warrant cards.

They indicated a seat on a sofa and took the seats opposite me.

'Mrs Latimer,' the woman began, 'we want you to know that we take allegations very seriously. Now, you're not in any trouble, but we called in at Malbister this afternoon and found the house bolted and the codes set to alert. We tried the communication button at the gates and we were patched through to a London number. According to the person we spoke with, the Goddard family have been at their London property for the past forty-eight hours.'

The man continued, 'We got a warrant to search the grounds and the security company came out to remove the chains from the front gates. We searched the buildings and outbuildings, including the old house and I'm sorry to say that we found no sign of your motorhome, or Mrs Goddard.'

'However,' the female officer said, 'your bag and your phone were handed in to the police this afternoon. Just be grateful that Caithness people are so honest. The items were found in the toilets of the Norseman Hotel, and the receptionist brought them up to the station just after

Malbister

lunchtime. '

'We've spoken to your husband and to your son, and there's a ticket waiting at Scrabster for the ferry to take you across to your son. The nurse in charge here says that you're making good progress and they'll discharge you after breakfast tomorrow.'

'You gave them time to cover their tracks,' I said, aware of the bitterness of my voice. 'I came in first thing this morning to tell you what I saw.'

'Mrs Latimer, these things take time. We had to get a warrant to enter Malbister estate. That meant we had to get the Justice of the Peace off his boat. That took the best part of two hours. Besides, with the blow you took to your head, you could well have been imagining what you saw.'

They handed over my bag and left, pausing to speak again to the nurses.

I had my phone, but no charger. The woman in the next bed, younger than me, and connected up to a drip, let me borrow hers. In the meantime, I went through my bag, checking my diary and my purse for anything that could be missing, or any clue to what was going on.

Once it was charged, I got out of bed, pulling the dressing gown around me, and padded through to the day room. I took a seat in the corner and rang Kevin.

'Wendy? Thank God. I was worried sick about you. The police rang me to say you'd been taken to hospital. I've been calling to find out how you are, and they said you'd had a brain scan or something?'

'It's a CT scan, dear. It's alright—I still have a brain,' I teased.

'So, what exactly is going on?' he asked.

I gave him a carefully edited version of events. A part of me hoped he was feeling guilty over my present state, but there was something I needed to ask him. 'That tracker you said was on my phone? Would it show where the phone was earlier today?'

He talked me through what to do. He told me that he loved me and that he wanted me to get home as soon as I could. 'No taking any silly risks, Wendy. I mean it. Come down to Devon and join me, once you get a bit of time with Matt.'

When I ended the call, I rang Matt and said that I had my bag back. 'Did you have time to cancel the cards?' I asked.

'No, Mum. The police rang to say your bag was found, so I thought I'd let you do that. I'm glad you've got your phone back. Is there any word about Aunt Kate?'

'No,' I said. 'The police needed to get a warrant and by the time they got the gates opened, the van and Katie were long gone. I'm going to have to leave it for now. I just want to see you tomorrow. Then I'll think what to do next.'

I sat in the comfortable chair, reluctant to return to the ward and to my hospital bed. I opened the settings icon on the iPhone and followed the instructions Kevin had given me. The phone was in Malbister this morning. It had been in Thurso mid-morning and several locations in Wick before it was left for a cleaner to find it in the hotel where I had worked with Joe only a few days before.

The last time I'd seen it, it was in the hands of Jack Goddard. Something wasn't adding up.

The nurse – a pleasant young woman in a starched white tunic – came looking for me, and ushered me into the shower and then back to bed, where she handed me tablets in a small paper cup and a plastic beaker of water. 'Paracetamol for your sore bits, and something to help you sleep,' she said.

Outside, the shadows lengthened and the sun dipped. In spite of my anguish over Kate, I drifted into an

Malbister

uncomfortable sleep, punctuated by disturbing and vivid dreams.

Chapter 50

14th June

I awoke in my hospital bed in a ward that was flooded by early sunlight and had to try to remember where I was and how I got here. I sat up in my bed when the breakfast ordered by the previous occupant of my bed arrived. Toast, butter and jam; a small carton of orange juice and a banana. The nurse came round to check on the patients and dish out medicine. I accepted my small cup with the two co-codamol and washed the caplets down with water from the jug on my bedside locker.

She made me wait until the doctor had done his mid-morning rounds before discharging me, snipping the plastic wristband. 'You took a right bang on the head, Wendy. See and take care of yourself,' she scolded. I took my soiled clothes from the locker, and went through to the shower room, trying to make myself look presentable. The auxiliary nurse, a cheerful woman with a short haircut and a wide smile, found me some shower gel and shampoo a patient had left behind, and a new toothbrush, and toothpaste, and I emerged feeling a bit more human.

Malbister

I rang the ferry company and checked the time of the sailings from Scrabster to Stromness, and then walked to the bus stance to check the bus times to Thurso. I wasn't comfortable wearing yesterday's pants, so I walked from the town to the vast Tesco on the road to John o Groats and bought a backpack and some cheap clothes and toiletries. Without my motorhome, I was literally starting from scratch. I changed my underwear in the supermarket toilets and applied some bronzer to my cheeks, and eyeliner pencil to make my eyes look less sleepy. At least my hair was clean, I thought as I tied it back with a clip.

I strolled back towards the town centre and wandered into the pedestrian precinct. It was lunchtime. I thought longingly of the French restaurant, but remembered there was a café at the harbour that looked nice, and would probably be cheaper. I was walking past a side street when I saw Morag, parked in a courtyard, with an open gate. Without thinking, I walked towards my van. The door was open. I looked around me, and walked towards my motorhome. I tried the door, and found it unlocked. I opened the driver's door and saw the key was in the ignition. There was no sign of Katie. I wondered if I should drive up to the police station and tell them that I'd recovered my property. The yard looked like it belonged to a tradesman—there were building materials stacked neatly at one end, and a small office.

I started the engine, and was about to reverse out of the yard when in the mirror I realised the yard gates were closing. I was trapped.

Chapter 51

The one person I'd not spoken to about my ordeal was my father. I'd told him I thought Kate was in danger before and he'd dismissed my fears. Now, trapped again, I thought back to how he always reacted if anything happened to either of his girls. He was too much of a buttoned-up bank branch manager to ever actually deck someone. His way of laying down the law involved filthy looks and an angry voice, which generally made whoever he was picking on back down. Right now, I reckoned, a bit of overreaction would come in handy. I roared my anger through the window at the men who approached the van, but realised they didn't understand a word I was saying. I recognised one of them as the Albanian farm worker who'd brought the bucket when Kate and I were in the cottage at Malbister.

My first instinct was to slam down the lock on my driver's side door, but the Albanian held the other key to my van and before I reacted to protect myself and my belongings, he'd unlocked the passenger side, clambered in and grabbed my bag, which I'd foolishly left on the passenger seat. His partner, grabbed me by my waistband and hauled me out of the van, pressing my head down to the

Malbister

cobblestones on the ground.

I tried fighting, lashing out at them with my flailing arms and legs, but there were two of them, and while they appeared to be weedy, they were stronger than they looked. And of course, it was pointless explaining that I'd already sustained a head injury and could they be a bit more careful where they were aiming their steel capped boots.

That damned van! If only I'd walked past the doorway, or even just taken out my phone and called the police? I could have been sitting in a window seat in Wickers World, tucking into a bowl of homemade soup and a sandwich. Instead, I was bound and gagged and thrown in the boot of an old Toyota, while my bag and my phone and Morag remained in the courtyard.

I heard the doors being dragged open and the Toyota engine spluttering into life. I hoped to goodness it didn't have a leaky exhaust. I presumed we were heading back to Malbister and I tried to brace myself against the back seats of the vehicle to avoid any more damage to my poor body. And to think I'd only just bought clean knickers!

While I'd walked all night to get to Wick, from Malbister, I knew the distance by car was less than half an hour. Sooner or later, they'd open the boot, and dispose of what was left of me. I wondered if they'd bury me under the trees, or throw my remains in a ditch? And who would tell Kevin and Matt and Amy what had become of me?

I tried counting to estimate the minutes, but half an hour passed and the Toyota engine continued to growl as we rumbled on. I felt sick, and worried about choking to death. I wondered if they'd let me out to pee, or to get some air at any point. I'd tried banging hard against the sides of the boot to get their attention, but they obviously weren't worried about delivering me to wherever we were going in one piece.

Julie MP Adams

After what felt about a couple of hours, they drew to a halt. I heard the handbrake being pulled on and one of them opened the boot. We were in a passing place and Morag was parked behind us.

The passenger from the front seat of the car hauled me out of the boot, and freed my feet. I was too stiff to run, and he ushered me into Morag and told me, in halting English, to use the loo. I had to manage with bound hands, but the sheer relief of being out of that coffin of a boot!

I pleaded with him through my gag not to put me back in the Toyota, and he indicated the bench seat of Morag, strapping me in and making sure my hands and feet were tied. The Toyota was being turned in the opposite direction and he climbed into the driver's seat and crunched the gears. I estimated we weren't far from Inverness and he was driving in a westerly direction. How on earth would Matt and Kevin ever find me now? I could only hope the tracker on my phone would lead them to me.

A small, still, internal voice chided me—while there's life, there's hope. And you need to find your sister. Out of the corner of my eye, I saw a butterfly settle on the back of the front passenger seat, and made myself breathe calmly through my nose. It gave me hope. I remembered the butterfly that showed me the escape route in the cottage, and prayed for a bit of strength to carry me through what lay ahead of me on this journey.

Chapter 52

I was right about our whereabouts and saw a sign pointing back towards Dingwall. We drove on narrow, winding roads, through the prettiest bit of the NC 500, taking the narrow road that passed through Garve, onto Achnasheen and onto the village of Shieldaig. As we left the east coast behind us, the mist crept in, and we were shrouded in haze.

In the camp sites, on my drive north, I'd heard talk of the challenge of driving Bealach Na Ba, the old cattle road, with the trickiest series of bends in the whole of Britain. It was nearby, and I hoped the man who was driving Morag rather badly, wasn't going to feel tempted to take it on.

In Sheildaig, we took a left turn onto an unmarked road. We bumped our way over a cattle grid, and then onto what was more of a track than a roadway. Finally, we stopped outside a long, low whitewashed cottage. My driver's understanding of English was poor, but we'd managed to communicate using sign language. Now, he picked up my handbag from the front passenger seat and climbed out the driver's side, and clumped his way towards the cottage.

He returned a few minutes later and untied my feet, hustling me out the back door of the van and pushing me towards the cottage. At the sage painted door, he gave me a push and I landed on my knees on a stone tiled floor, looking up at Judith Goddard.

Her grey bob was carefully combed, and her habitual black clothes were expensive, elegant and exquisitely cut. Her sharp eyes were carefully made up and there were jet drops in her ears. I could smell her lavender and citrus scent. She was cool, clean and in command. In contrast I was a crumpled and broken mess.

'Thank you, Agron,' she said, handing him an envelope. He opened it, and I could see a wad of bank notes inside. He lurched off in the direction of a caravan to the side of the cottage.

I stumbled to my feet and checked myself over, as best I could.

'Well, Wendy Latimer,' she said. 'You really are an irritating woman. I gave you so many chances to avoid this. Your interfering has made things a great deal worse for you and for your sister.' She made no attempt to untie my gag or my hands, instead, pushing me onto a sofa.

'What am I going to do with you?' she mused.

The cottage probably housed a family of eight, in Victorian times, but it was extensively and recently renovated. The walls were insulated and plastered and this part, which served as hall, sitting room, dining room and kitchen was painted white. It was the opposite of Malbister—this was a pleasingly proportioned space. The builder's wife in me couldn't help liking the dark grey kitchen units, and the open shelves stacked with rustic stoneware that probably cost a fortune. There was a round scrubbed pine kitchen table with four chairs, and I was sitting on one of two small sofas, arranged in front of a wood burning stove with an Ercol coffee table on a blue grey tartan rug between

Malbister

them.

The cottage walls were at least a foot thick: there were bench seats in the two windows in the sitting area. Behind the sofa where Judith now perched was a gallery wall devoted to her family, with more photographs and tartan lamp bases with duck egg blue shades on the low shelves either side of the chimney breast. Plump blue grey tweed cushions punctuated the sofas, and a large candle bowl with three wicks sat on the coffee table. Under normal circumstances, I'd have been complimenting my hostess on her impeccable decorating tastes. It was hard to do so with a gag in my mouth. I sat helpless on her sofa. The only bright side was that I wasn't chained to a rusty old bed in a hovel. Yet.

I've always needed specs to read, but there's nothing wrong with my distance vision. I looked at the photographs behind Judith Goddard. Most of them featured her Bluebeard of a son, and the more recent ones included Jack and the poisonous twins. I noticed that only one showed one of her three daughters in law – the wedding picture of Fiona and Malcolm.

She saw me looking at that one, and her eyes narrowed. I felt I was in this enclosed space with a she wolf, and I was dinner.

I was terrified. Where was my sister?

Chapter 53

A door at the rear of the kitchen led to the rest of the cottage. I squirmed and indicated by a series of grunts that I needed to go to the bathroom. My hands still bound, I wriggled to my feet and followed her through the door, wondering if I could take her by surprise? Through the doorway was a narrow corridor with three identical doors. She opened the middle one and pushed me into a tiny, chalk white bathroom. She said 'Don't try anything. I will be waiting outside.'

One of the things I've learned over the years, working in a department store, is that you learn a lot about people from the small, personal things they buy. Malbister was over sized, from the huge windows to the vast sofas. The cupboards were full of designer goods that nobody used. It was ostentation, and lacking in taste.

When I first entered this cottage, my first thought was it must be a holiday rental. The gallery of family pictures convinced me otherwise. This looked more like a home than Malbister could ever be. I used the toilet, but didn't press the button to flush, giving me time to look in the cabinets, using my bound hands to open them. The few toiletries were mainly Childs Farm unscented stuff. There was an electric

Malbister

toothbrush and toothpaste for sensitive teeth, dental floss and a packet of temazepam tablets. I wondered if that was what she used when she drugged our water? I tugged at my gag, but with my wrists bound together, I had no means of loosening it. I badly needed a drink of water, so I moistened the fabric, in the hope of getting some of the precious liquid into my mouth. My head started to throb again. She rapped at the door, and I flushed the toilet and went out into the corridor. She hesitated for a moment, and then opened a second door and pushed me inside.

The room must be the one used by the twins. It was big enough for two single beds with a tiny chest of drawers between them. Katie lay in one and I was pushed onto the other.

Each bed was covered by a single duvet in a white cotton cover, with a plaid blanket neatly folded at the foot. The window, I noticed, was double glazed and locked shut. I heard her slide the bolt to lock us in.

Kate lay on her back, and I saw her arm was in a makeshift sling, and she was wearing clean pyjamas. At least Judith tried to make her comfortable, I thought. I called her name. 'Kate? Can you hear me, Katie? It's Wendy.'

She stirred, but didn't wake up. I looked out of the small window. The mist obscured the sun, and while it was late afternoon, I couldn't see much of the landscape surrounding us. Where was this place exactly? And what did Judith Goddard have planned for us?

Chapter 54

I spent the next few hours trying to loosen my gag, and to ease the bonds round my hands. My captors were pretty adept at tying people up, but gradually, little by little, I worked at the knots on the gag, and finally managed to spit the fabric out. Then, using my teeth, I worked to free my hands. I looked around for anything I could use to defend us, should the she wolf send her thugs in to torment us again.

Kate moaned in her sleep, and I put a hand on her head and murmured softly to her, 'It's okay, Katie, I'm here. Wendy's here.'

Later, she woke up and started in fright. 'Oh, Wendy, they didn't get you too?'

I said, 'You didn't think I would leave you, did you? I went to the police, but they wasted time getting anyone out to rescue you, and then they made me spend the night in hospital. This morning, I saw Morag in a yard and went in to take it back, and that's when they caught me.'

She groaned. 'We're done for. She'll never let us leave. She's insane.'

'What is this place, Kate? And why did she bring us here?'

Kate moved her arm and almost screamed in pain. 'It's

Malbister

Malcolm's old home. Judith's parents lived here when he was small. She used to bring him here in school holidays. Malcolm had it done up a few months ago, to try to persuade her to come back here to live.'

'You didn't say that before? You mean he wanted her to live here? I got the impression that she was in charge of the family.'

'That's the problem,' she replied. 'Do you remember how Dad was with us? How he used to bully Mum?'

I looked down at my hands and the marks on my wrists. I thought of all of the things that our darling Mum missed out on, because Dad wasn't interested in them or refused to pay for them. He was a bully, and capable of taking any occasion and making it into a complete misery. I'd assumed Malcolm was Katie's way of marrying Daddy. Had I been wrong?

The door opened and Judith Goddard stood there. She glanced at my hands and my mouth, free of their bonds. I was damned if I was going to let her try to silence me again or tie me up.

To my surprise, she indicated the corridor and ushered us both into the kitchen. The table was laid for three and there was a delicious smell coming from the Aga.

She took a bottle of red wine and deftly removed the cork with an ancient corkscrew. She poured three glasses and set one at each place. We looked at one another. What on earth was she up to now?

I worked out that if I waited until she took a mouthful of wine or a forkful of food that it would be safe to eat. We sat down, and she set a dish of home-made lasagne and another of salad on the table, and indicated we should serve ourselves. I got up to fetch a glass of water from the tap and she glowered at me.

'By this time tomorrow, you will both be out of my way,' she said. 'I thought you deserved a last supper.' She got up and fetched a dish of garlic bread. I waited until she served herself and took a bite from the bread before beginning mine, and I waited until she had taken a drink before starting my wine, which was delicious.

'Judith,' I began, watching her start at my use of her name. 'Why do you hate us so much?'

She took a forkful of salad, put it in her mouth and chewed carefully before replying. 'I neither hate nor like you, Mrs Latimer. You simply get in my way.'

Katie watched us both nervously. I pushed on, 'What has Katie ever done to deserve being locked up and tortured? If you want rid of us, why not simply open the door and let us go? Let me take both of us back south, and you'll never need to see either of us again.'

My frightened rabbit of a sister nibbled at a lettuce leaf, quivering with fear. This was not good.

'Look around you, Mrs Latimer,' Judith said, indicating the cottage's lovely interior with a sweep of her arm. 'What do you see?'

This was a bear trap of a conversation. I took a spoon of lasagne, and savoured its garlic, smoky taste. No matter how she treated her house guests, she could certainly cook. 'It's a lovely cottage,' I observed.

'This was my home when I was a child. In those days it was smaller and there was no running water or bathroom. My family were not rich—my father was a farm servant. I was working at the hunting lodge on the estate in my school holidays, when one of the laird's party thought it would be fun to have his way with me,' she began. 'I was a fifteen-year-old girl, helping out as a waitress. Malcolm was born nine months later. My father threw me out, and wanted my son

Malbister

to be adopted. He apologised to the laird for my immorality,' she said bitterly.

'That's dreadful,' I replied, meaning it. 'It wasn't your fault. The man who did that to you should have been in trouble – not you.'

She grimaced. 'He was young, wealthy and entitled. I was under age and his family made sure he refused consent to put his name on Malcolm's birth certificate. I had to put 'father unknown', as if I was a trollop. I'd given birth in an awful mother and baby home, and my parents refused to take me back. The laird, it seemed, found me an embarrassment, and had I returned, my parents would have been turned out of their home and lost their jobs. They were too scared to have me return with a baby.'

I thought back—this must have been in the late 1960's. At that time, she could have had a termination, I thought, and then remembered with a pang how I'd dreaded that date at the clinic, and been saved from the decision by Kevin. Having someone to stand by you made a world of difference.

'How did you survive?' I asked.

'I saw an advertisement for an au pair, in the Scotsman. The family wanted a Scottish girl, and they were prepared for me to bring my baby with me. The husband was a schoolmaster, and he and his wife were childless. She was an alcoholic, and he needed the house to be clean and tidy.'

'Mr Goddard?' I asked.

She nodded.

'I saw Malcolm's birth father at a sports day, along with other Old Boys. His younger brother was at the school,' she said. The bitterness in her voice was clear.

'How did he react to seeing you and his son?' I asked.

She ignored my question, instead continuing, 'By that time, my employer's wife was dying of liver cancer, and when she passed, Eton frowned on a master having a single woman with her child in his house, and he suggested he make an honest woman of me and adopt Malcolm.'

Katie was listening carefully, but leaving it to me to prompt. It was the most I'd heard Judith speak, and I almost felt sorry for her.

'We were married for almost twelve years,' she said. 'He died when Malcolm was about to start his place at Eton. He'd paid for me to have music lessons, and after he died, and we lost the house, Malcolm became a boarder and I was given a room and a job as a violin instructor.

'You have to understand, Mrs Latimer, that I was determined that my son should have his birth right, and I did everything I could to make sure of his education and his place in the world. I knew that when he was a man, making his way in the world, that he would remember my sacrifices.'

Katie spoke. 'And he bought the estate and gave you this lovely cottage, to show his gratitude.'

It was the wrong thing to say. Judith Goddard narrowed her eyes and slammed her glass down on the table so hard I expected it to smash.

'He wanted to send me back where I came from. He was telling me that he no longer needed me. I was being made redundant,' she snarled.

I privately thought being redundant with a free house was a damn sight better than being out of work and living in an old campervan, but I kept that to myself and said, 'Your son has always needed you, Mrs Goddard. You raised his children, after all?'

'When he married Fiona,' she said, 'he'd arrived and taken his proper place in the world. She was from the same class as his natural father. My boy was clever and talented and married to an aristocrat. When Jack was born, I was the

Malbister

happiest of women.' She had drifted away into a happier time, and I only hoped she was going to extend a bit of compassion to us.

'Malcolm always asked me along, when they went on holiday. Jack had nannies, but they came and went, and I was always happy to lend a hand. By then, I'd left Eton, and gave music lessons from my flat. But then, on that skiing trip I heard my daughter in law laugh about me behind my back. She had the neck to accuse Malcolm of having an Oedipus complex. She spoke about getting rid of the old dragon.'

Katie looked down at her plate. She'd hardly touched her lasagne, while Judith had taken a few forkfuls, and I'd eaten most of mine. Judith was telling us how she'd dealt with the first wife. I wondered if I could get to the knife block – but then remembered Agran who was probably standing sentry outside. It was still daylight, and the mist was lifting gradually, warming up the evening light in the white room.

'I saw her the next day on the slopes, clowning around with some other people. One of them was Malcolm's real father. I watched him kissing her. She was betraying my son and my grandson. I decided to put a stop to it, even if it meant my being killed in the process.

'Of course,' she continued, 'it was a tragic accident. Fiona seemed unharmed at first, while I was packed off to hospital with a broken collarbone and a smashed femur. And then later in the day, it turned out she had a bleed on her brain and died.'

'Malcolm needed me more than ever,' she said, gathering up the plates and taking them to the sink. 'No, Wendy, I can manage,' she said, loading the dishwasher. 'Can't have you getting too close to the knives. Not with what I'm confessing.'

She returned to the table and poured herself another

glass of wine. 'I moved in with him and Jack and we were a happy little family again. The insurance money meant he had the means to live like a gentleman. But the next I knew, he was cajoled into making up numbers on another skiing holiday, and when he returned, the silly boy told me he was madly in love.'

That must have been Maria Gambini, I thought.

'He loved her more than she loved him,' Judith Goddard said. 'I was sure of that. They couldn't keep their hands off one another and the twins were on their way, so I couldn't stop the marriage, but I persuaded her parents that a grand wedding was out of the question.'

'But wasn't it a good thing that he was in love?' I asked, cursing myself the moment the words were out. Judith was clearly unhinged, and it was unwise to provoke her.

'I made it clear that I was there for both of them,' she said. 'And when she was mentally ill, I was there to help with the babies.'

'What happened to her?' I asked. I'd heard Thalia Gambini's side of the story, but if Judith Goddard was in confessional mode, this might be the only chance for the truth to be told – if of course, either Kate or I survived.

'Her sister turned up, to help her pack her bags and take the twins away. We were in Caithness. Malcolm was hosting a shooting party for his company. While the men were on the moors, I caught them loading the babies into her sister's car. I caught them, and ordered the sister to go and leave Maria and the babies behind. She went willingly. I can be merciful, Wendy.'

'We had words, and I'm afraid I convinced Maria that she was an unfit mother. She went up to bed that night and took an overdose. When Malcolm left for a business trip the next day, I told him Maria was resting.

Malbister

'The insurance company would not pay out in the event of a suicide. I buried her under the trees and returned to London with the babies. I dressed in her clothes and got on a train. I took off the cap and coat before I got off the train and told the police she left the house and never came back. After seven years, she was declared legally dead. I had my son, and my grandchildren. And then' she said, looking at Kate, 'he met you.'

'Malcolm bought this estate and decorated this cottage and handed me the keys to my own prison a fortnight ago. I'd worked on the children, and told them that their new stepmother wanted rid of them. I told the twins that their stepmother wanted to send them to live with the aunt I made sure they never met. I convinced Jack that his allowance was going to be stopped. They were very happy to help their old grandmother. After all, I was always there for them, and I have their best interests at heart.'

'What about Joe?' I asked. 'What did he ever do to you?'

'That fool?' she said. 'Always under his wife's thumb? He stopped Malcolm getting Maria's share of the Gambini company for the twins. He rode to the rescue of this worthless creature, and he was getting in our way. Jack shot him, and I told the police that the Shaikhs had a guard and diplomatic immunity. They cannot prove otherwise, unless Kate tells the police.'

She stood up and went across to the fridge, and took out a large cheesecake. 'Well, ladies, how about some dessert?'

Chapter 55

I couldn't swallow a mouthful of the cheesecake. We'd just heard that woman confess to three deaths. She'd as good as killed Maria Gambini, and she'd got her grandson to kill Joe and attack us. She'd made her own grandchild into a cold-hearted killer.

There was no way she was going to allow either of us to live. Katie's husband loved her—but his mother was turning his family into monsters. She stopped Kate having the wedding Mum longed for her to have. She robbed me of the last few precious weeks with a mother I loved.

This hatchet-faced harpy was intent on committing murder and I was under no illusions. This was probably going to be the last night of my life. I thought of Matt and Amy and Kevin, and I wondered what tale she would spin to account for our demise.

'I think we won't need any coffee,' she said. Then she opened the door, and ushered us out. No doubt, I reckoned, we'd be dragged into the caravan and left to die slowly after our last supper.

Instead, she walked across to Morag and unlocked the passenger side. She took my phone out of my bag, threw it

Malbister

on the ground and stamped on it. Then she threw the keys to me. 'Take this thing out of my sight, and take your sister with you,' she snarled, before turning on her heel, marching to the cottage and slamming the door behind her.

Kate got into the passenger seat as quietly as a lamb. I bent down to pick up my broken phone, before climbing into the driver's seat and fastening my seat belt. This was too good to be true. I turned Morag carefully. I realised, as we trundled down the road that we were heading for Bealach na Ba, the highlight of the NC500, and I wondered what Judith Goddard had done to my van.

Chapter 56

What can I say about Bealach na Ba? It is ten miles of heaven or hell, depending on how strong your nerves are. Once, it was the only route connecting Applecross to the outside world. These days there's another road that hugs the coast to the north – the route I'd travelled on earlier. The Bealach na Ba was originally a cattle track and later, in the 1950's it was turned into a narrow tarmac road with hairpin bends and a few passing places. It's like a gigantic bowl, with mountains to one side and on the other, the road, which sticks to a high cliff with crash barriers to prevent the foolhardy falling to their deaths. Even then, it is the last place on earth you want to meet a big vehicle coming the other way. It's one of the steepest roads in the country with a gradient that makes it completely unsuitable for heavy vehicles. Near the viewpoint, there are about half a dozen very tight hairpin bends, that make the Berriedale Braes in Caithness look like a motorway. If you are descending, you need to take these hairpin bends very, very carefully. If there's something coming up the hill, even if it's a cyclist or a hiker, the gap between you, and them and the crash barrier is terrifyingly narrow.

Malbister

It is a road you should only take in daylight and avoid if it's getting dark, or misty, or if you've drunk two glasses of wine and sustained a head injury over the previous 48 hours.

Worse still, is if you are forced to take this road in a motorhome which has a brake light coming on.

The Albanians had blocked access to the other road, forcing us on to Bealach. I looked at Kate, shivering with fear in the passenger seat. 'It's okay, Katie,' I tried to reassure her. 'I've got this.'

Now, all I had to do was convince myself.

'Kate, who were you arguing with when you made that but call?' It was the question I'd wanted to ask for ten days, and given we were probably going to be killed, I reckoned it was time my sister gave me a straight answer.

'Malcolm arranged a dinner party to celebrate buying the cottage. He'd got me to buy a special gift box and we wrapped the key to the cottage in it, with tartan ribbon. It was going to be a surprise. He'd stayed with his grandparents on holidays from Eton, and loved it, and he thought he was doing his mum a huge favour, giving her a place of her own. Tonight, was the first I'd heard of his birth—I'd always assumed his father was his mother's husband.'

'No wonder she went off the edge, Kate,' I replied. 'It would have been the last place on earth I'd have wanted to live. But why wait so long to tell you? Does Malcolm know?'

She shrugged. 'She had a row with him. I didn't hear what it was about, because she marched him into the office and slammed the door. I caught the twins trying to listen, and when it was over and he came out, he snapped at me.'

'Did that happen a lot? Snapping at you?'

'It didn't at first. When it was just the two of us, he was lovely. Kind, caring, and I thought it would always be like that. When the twins and Jack were around, I was always in the wrong. Judith always pulled the strings. Wendy—what's that light?'

I knew it. The brake light warning was flashing. I pushed my foot down on the brake and it didn't feel right. Worse still, the truck the Albanians used to block the safer road was now bearing down on us from behind.

I could only hope I could lower my speed enough to get us into a passing place, but what would they do to us then? Judith was covering her tracks. She didn't want us dead on her own doorstep. Instead, she sent us on to the most dangerous road in Britain with broken brakes, and no way of calling for help.

Chapter 57

I'd had a road accident shortly after I passed my driving test, and lost my confidence behind the wheel. Kevin's friend Barry, who was in the police, told me to do the Institute of Advanced Motorists test. I'd learned a lot at the time, then forgot it all—mainly because Kevin was always there to do the driving and I tended to be in the passenger seat. Now, I racked my brains to remember what to do in the event of a crisis. I couldn't afford to lose any of my concentration now. My head was aching but I was running on pure adrenaline.

The first thing I needed to do was to lower my gears, and bring my speed down that way. The notorious hairpin bends were approaching, with that terrifying sheer drop to one side. I prayed there was nothing coming in the other direction—but all the while that truck behind me was nudging closer to Morag's rear bumper.

I clung to the steering wheel as if my life depended on it—which literally it did. As the first bend approached, I got down to second gear and carefully navigated around it, aware that I wasn't going to be able to stop and reverse if I judged it wrong. Kate's hurt arm meant she couldn't even cling to the grab handle and she pressed her back into the seat.

I was silently praying as each successive bend approached, pulling the gears down to second and then down to first, to bring us round safely. I was averaging a speed of under thirty miles an hour on the straight sections, and trying to get down as low as possible for the bends.

I did a deal with whoever was up there. Get Katie and me to safety and I promise to be good for the rest of my life. I'd make my peace with Kevin and cherish every moment I had with Matt and Amy. Just please keep them safe and out of the clutches of Judith Goddard.

The next bend was a nightmare, with a sheer drop to the side. Katie had her eyes shut tight, and I knew she was praying. I had to keep my eyes glued to the road and try not to think of the drop to the side of the crash barriers. I felt the sickening crunch as the truck behind nudged Morag and we swung out, glancing against the barrier, before I got the steering back under control, and continued on, dropping gear to second.

The truck repeated that manoeuvre on the next bend and as we were approaching the third, I saw the cyclist.

He was clad in bright yellow lycra, with a yellow helmet, and I was terrified he was going to brake, go over his handlebars and fall to his death. Mercifully, I swung Morag into the passing place and saw him avoid the truck. My heart was racing and as the next bend approached, the truck struck us again, then to my horror, it crashed into the barrier.

I forced myself to keep my eyes on the road, and not to look in the mirror. I got us round the remaining bends, aware we were no longer being pursued. The final tricky bend was ahead of us, and beyond that the road crossed moorland. I lowered gear again, and got Morag round, and onto the straight stretch ahead.

Finally, heart pounding, we approached Strathcarron. I

Malbister

dropped gear and steered into a driveway and pulled on the handbrake and cut the engine. We'd survived.

Chapter 58

We prepared to spend the night in Morag. I made Kate comfortable on the double bed and swung myself into the over-cab bunk. We were both exhausted and Kate was in agony. I cursed the broken phone. All I could hope was that the tracker was still working. And that Judith wouldn't take it into her head to come and attack us in the night.

Come morning, I'd try to find a land line and call for help.

We didn't have to wait that long. The sun dipped below the horizon and rose again, and as the birds began their chorus, a police patrol car pulled in beside us. Linda MacLeod got out of the back seat.

I was relieved to see her. For once she was less than immaculate, in jeans and a t shirt and her hair loose over her shoulders. She looked as if she'd been summoned from her bed. She rubbed her eyes sleepily and yawned, showing perfect white teeth.

'Well, Mrs Latimer, and Mrs Goddard. What have you been doing?'

The cyclist witnessed the truck hitting Morag and then going over the crash barrier. He needed to wait for his descent to Applecross to get a mobile signal to call it in. While we'd slept, the mountain rescue team were summoned to check for survivors. Miraculously the Albanians sustained injuries that were not life threatening. Judith Goddard, in the back seat, without a seatbelt had not been so lucky. We'd missed the comings and goings of the air ambulance that took her to Raigmore then on to Glasgow.

I told MacLeod and the patrol men about the sabotaged brakes and she whistled through her teeth. 'You did Bealach Na Ba in a motorhome without brakes and lived? God, that's one for the NC500 book of legends. But, right now, we need to get your sister to hospital, and I'll need witness statements from both of you.'

One of the patrolmen got out of the car, and MacLeod took his place in the front passenger seat, with Kate and myself in the back seats. The driver muttered about Broadford hospital in Skye being closer and we drove to Kyle of Lochalsh and over the bridge to Skye.

In the Accident and Emergency department of the Dr McKinnon hospital, they triaged Katie and looked at my head injury, and decided we both needed to go to Raigmore. The ambulance was already deployed for the two Albanians, so we were returned to the patrol car and driven to Raigmore, with DCI MacLeod itching to start interviewing us.

Raigmore – a massive concrete expanse of hospital – swallowed us up into its functioning heart, and Kate was whipped off to Radiography, returning with a diagnosis of a dislocated collar bone and a hairline fracture of the wrist. They admitted her as an inpatient, but reckoned she'd be discharged within twenty-four hours. The registrar on duty looked at my head and prescribed rest. MacLeod told me to book myself into a cheap hotel and turn up at police HQ for questioning in the afternoon.

I took my broken phone into a repair shop, where it was pronounced dead on arrival. The lad behind the counter removed my SIM and suggested I bought a cheap replacement in the Eastgate Centre. Once that was done, I rang Matt.

'Mum! Where the heck are you? I've been worried sick. I waited for every ferry, and I was scared stiff for you.'

'Matt, I'm in Inverness. Your aunt Kate is in Raigmore Hospital and I'm going to be stuck in Inverness for the time being. Morag's a bit the worse for wear, though,' I admitted, thinking of my valiant motorhome being uplifted by the AA.

'As long as you're in one piece, I'm fine with that, Mum,' he said. 'What are the police saying?'

'Not very much, yet,' I admitted. 'I've to go in for questioning, this afternoon. Let's just say it's been a bit of a dramatic day or so, lately. I'll ring you later.'

I managed to get 4G on the phone and booked myself into the Travelodge in the town centre. Now, I had to gather up what Kate and I would need to get us through the next twenty-four hours. That meant buying more knickers and toothpaste and cheap summer clothes in Primark.

I checked in at the Travelodge and treated myself to a hot shower and a change of clothes. I needed to be at the police station for three, but on the way, I went into Debenhams, and used the testers at the Dior counter to make me look human again. I sprayed myself liberally with the tester for Chanel 5, put my handbag across my body, and set off to meet DCI MacLeod.

Outside the police station, I noticed a man and a woman deep in conversation. At first, I didn't recognise Thalia Gambini, but the man was the peat cutter I'd seen outside Malbister. He looked different, with neat hair and smarter clothes.

I gave my name to the woman at the front desk and she buzzed the intercom through to tell DCI MacLeod that I was in reception. MacLeod popped her head outside a swing door and told me to come through to an interview room. MacLean was already there, preparing the recording machinery.

'How's your sister?' she asked. I noticed she'd obviously gone home to change—she wore her black linen suit, and her hair was back in its clamp.

'She's being kept in overnight,' I said. 'Has anyone rung her husband yet?'

'Ah, the missing Mr Goddard,' she remarked.

'Was that Thalia Richards, I saw outside, just now?' I asked.

She nodded. 'Mrs Richards has been very helpful,' she said, 'As has Rory Sutherland.'

The peat cutter. The one who showed me the way into Malbister. I could have done with him being a bit more helpful, I thought. He'd sent me into danger, and didn't hang about to see if either Kate or myself needed rescuing.

'Hang about,' I began, 'I thought he used to work for the Malbister estate? I met him outside the gates and he told me how to get through the gap in the hedge. He knew I'd be in trouble if I was caught, and he didn't lift a finger to help me.'

MacLean had been eating again. There were crumbs on his tie, and he burped, loudly, and apologised. 'He used to work on the estate. These days he's some sort of private investigator. Mrs Richards had him making enquiries about her sister. He was working under cover. He witnessed her husband's murder. It's blown the story of the accidental shooting by foreign security personnel right out of the water. The Home Secretary is furious—Goddard is a major donor

Julie MP Adams

to the Conservative Party, and having his son arrested for murder, in addition to wasting the time of the security services, is a serious embarrassment.'

'Right, Mrs Latimer,' DCI MacLeod said, looking at her watch. 'We need to know everything that happened to you from the moment you left Caithness General Hospital in Wick.'

I told them about walking to the café, and seeing Morag parked in that yard. I described how I was seized and bound and gagged and stuffed in the boot of the Toyota. I told them about being driven to Applecross and about the cottage, and that dinner, where Judith Goddard revealed her dark secrets, while she fed us what was supposed to be our last supper. I described how she packed us off in Morag, making sure we would have to tackle Bealach na Ba, as the fluid leaked from our brakes.

'Hmm, driving while drunk, and in a defective vehicle? You do realise we will need to charge you, Mrs Latimer.'

'Even though we were coerced?' I asked.

'You could have locked yourself in and stayed put,' she replied. 'However, we have a translator working with the Albanians and they confirm your story. Mrs Goddard promised them your motorhome, and they were changing the number plates when you interrupted them.'

'They were driving a truck behind me and trying to drive us off the road,' I reminded her. She then made me go into details of everything I could remember and she said that when Kate was strong enough to leave hospital, she would need to corroborate my account.

'What happened to Judith Goddard?' I asked.

'She's not in a good way,' MacLeod said. 'She was talkative while the mountain rescue people were there, but she lost consciousness in the air ambulance and she's

Malbister

currently in intensive care in Glasgow. It's touch and go whether she will live.'

'Right, Mrs Latimer,' she said at last. 'I you to read back and sign your witness statement and then I think you are free to go.' She stood up and showed me out of the interview room, through reception and out the front door.

Chapter 59

Kate was sitting up in bed, but no longer groaning in pain. I wondered what the doctors had given her for pain relief? I handed over the bag with toiletries and clothes. She'd normally never been seen dead in anything from Primark, but right now, she was simply relieved to be alive.

'Have you spoken to Malcolm?' I asked.

'Can you pour me a glass of water, please?' she asked and I did so and placed the plastic glass in her good hand.

'He's having to get lawyers to deal with Jack,' she began. 'He's going to be charged with murder, so I think I'm the last thing on his mind, right now. After that, he's going to need to see to his mother.'

'When you get out of here, where are you going to go?' I asked.

'The twins are going to need him,' she said. 'If Judith dies, they'll have a lot of adjusting to do, and right now, I don't think they want me around. I've rung Dad and said I'm going to rent an apartment near him for a month. Fancy coming with me? I think after all of this, you could use a holiday.'

I smiled. 'If that's an invitation, I'm going to say thank

Malbister

you, and I accept.'

Epilogue

December 2019

I'd set out on my journey determined that it was going to be the start of a new chapter in my life. My home was gone, and the job I'd grown accustomed to doing. I wasn't sure that there was any mileage left in my marriage.

Kate and I spent a month with Dad, and Patsy, Mum's friend—a jolly widow who took no nonsense from him. Kate spent much of the time singing my praises and telling the story of our torment at the hands of Judith Goddard.

Against all the odds, Judith survived, but was confined to a wheelchair. Her loving son hired a team of doctors to demonstrate she was in no fit state to stand trial. Then he sent her on a round the world cruise. 'It's better than being in a care home,' he told Kate. 'She'll have meals and entertainment and a nurse. And it means I don't have to set eyes on her.'

The twins spent the rest of that summer getting to know their aunt Thalia, in Venice.

Jack was going to be charged with murder, but the evidence given about his grandmother's malign influence

Malbister

allowed a plea bargain to reduce the charge to manslaughter. Rory Sutherland's eye witness statement, together with forensic evidence meant a guilty plea was his only option. I hear he's not been a model prisoner, though, and the outside world is a better place without him.

Matt and Freya both began their doctorates and I'm hoping they don't take too long to realise they are made for one another.

Morag was repaired and the AA delivered her back to my friend Dorothy's driveway, where I picked her up after my return from Spain. I started my course in Sheffield in September, and I should complete it next summer.

I know what you want to ask me. What happened with Kevin?

I went down to Devon when I got back, and saw the prototype he'd worked on for Joe Ricci complete. It was every bit as nice as the CAD drawings in those brochures. There's a patent in process—which will be in Thalia's name, but JTC Holdings are going ahead with the project and Kevin and the lads have the contract to build the mobile lodges. There's going to be several sites – Devon, Cornwall and Applecross. Malcolm Goddard has leased the land around the cottage to the company.

Once I complete the course, I've got a contract as project manager, and I'm going to be my husband's boss. After this summer, I've no doubt I'm more than up to the job. Kevin is perfectly happy with the arrangement. And so am I.

Acknowledgements

I freely admit that I write the way that other people knit—and this novel was intended to be a Christmas gift for my friends. I spent four decades teaching English, and getting something in print was something I wanted to do but never quite managed. The challenge was set for me by my friend and lateral thinking guru, Giacchino Livoti, to stop me moaning about wanting to write and do something about it. Over the past two years, I've written a topical short story every Christmas and sent it out in lieu of a newsletter. This time, thanks to Covid lockdowns, I've managed to produce first drafts of not one but two novels.

I'd like to thank Gordon Phillips for his guide to tackling the notorious Bealach na Ba – which I almost drove on one of my road trips with my Dad. The North Coast 500 has this as one of its highlights, but I wanted to show that there's more to the route than just a fast drive around the North Highlands.

Much of this book is my way of saying thank you to the place where I lived for four decades of my life – the county of Caithness. Often overlooked by those rushing round the NC500, Wick, in particular is well worth a visit, and I can guarantee if you eat out there, you will eat extremely well, as Wendy and Thalia's visit to my favourite French restaurant, Bord de L'Eau demonstrates. Danny and Janice are total stars and I still dream about that wonderful salmon starter.

Thank you to my friends and fellow retired teachers for reading the first drafts – to Heather, Rena, Pat, Kathryn, Marjory, Sheila, Grace and Diana.

Thanks also to my walking companions, Susan, Vaila, Willi, Kirsten, Gail and Garry, who got me out into the open air, where all the best plotting is done.

A huge thanks to the proper writers on Twitter – Marion

Todd, Olga Voytas and Brian R Stewart, for showing me the way, and to Dawn Geddes for her tutorials on the business of being a writer.

And finally, a huge thankyou to Fraser and Sandra, and to my study buddy, Barrie – whose constant encouragement is a true blessing.

About the Author

Julie MP Adams is an East Coast Scot, who lived on the NC500 route for many years. An unrepentant gate crasher, she was a folk singer, student journalist and a civil servant before embarking on a long career in education. Currently she is a writer and blogger, and a walk leader with Paths for All. She (normally) loves theatre, film and live music.

Printed in Great Britain
by Amazon